SPOILT ROYALS

Alan MacDonald

Illustrated by
Tony Reeve

Hippo

Scholastic Children's Books
Commonwealth House, 1–19 New Oxford Street,
London WC1A 1NU, UK

A division of Scholastic Limited
London ~ New York ~ Toronto ~ Sydney ~ Auckland
Mexico City ~ New Delhi ~ Hong Kong

Published in the UK by Scholastic Ltd, 1999

Text copyright © Alan MacDonald, 1999
Illustrations copyright © Tony Reeve, 1999

ISBN 0 590 11249 X

All rights reserved
Typeset by TW Typesetting, Midsomer Norton, Somerset
Printed by Cox & Wyman Ltd, Reading, Berks.

10 9 8 7 6 5 4 3 2

The right of Alan MacDonald and Tony Reeve to be identified
as the author and illustrator of this work respectively has been
asserted by them in accordance with the Copyright, Designs and
Patents Act, 1988.

SPOILT
ROYALS

Contents

SO YOU WANT TO BE ROYAL?

Do you ever dream that life could be different? That you could be rich, famous and powerful? That you could hit the headlines? Look no further.

WANTED: ROYALTY

Hugely ambitious person wanted to sit on the British Throne

Qualifications: Blue blood, toffee nose, plum in the mouth.

Salary: Outrageous.

Duties: Travel by private yacht, train or jet all over the world, wave at people, shake hands with presidents, sultans, kings etc. Look good on stamps and banknotes. Must be able to ride horses and take corgis for walks.

Perks of the job: Live-in accommodation (choose from half a dozen palaces), armies of toadying servants, your own coat of arms and a year's supply of headscarves. Send letter of application and photo – in profile – to the House of Windsor. No commoners, please.

ME! ME! I'LL DO IT. KING DAN THE FIRST.

Sorry, only kidding. Adverts like this never appear in newspapers. You can't join the royal family by applying for the job. The royals call themselves "The Firm" but they like to keep the business in the family. It's not surprising when you realize that the Queen is probably the richest woman in the world. Be honest. If you were stinking rich would you advertise for people to help you spend your lolly?

The fact is royals are spoilt. They can do whatever they like. Did you know if the Queen wanted, she could do any of these things tomorrow? (In her dreams anyway.)

1 Sack the government.

2 Declare war.

3 Make a few more knights.

4 Pardon everyone in prison (on the Prime Minister's advice, of course).

5 Sell Balmoral to buy more racehorses.

So who says royals don't have any power anymore? Just think, you could go to school tomorrow and find you have to call your teacher Lord Peabody instead of "sir".

Being spoilt rotten, the royals aren't eager to share their power and wealth with anybody else.

Get royal

There are ways to become a royal – some fair, some foul. Most have been tried before. You can choose from succession, murder, marriage or Monopoly. (Spot the one that hasn't been tried before.)

1 Succession

Firstly you could succeed to the throne. This is the normal route to becoming king or queen of England. It has a long and not-so-glorious history.

This is how succession works...

If you are the queen's eldest son then you're next in line when she pops her royal clogs.

NICE ONE, YOUR MAJESTY

Good job you're not the eldest daughter.

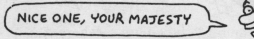

WHY'S THAT?

Because girls don't count the same as boys.

WAIT A MINUTE, THE QUEEN IS A GIRL. OR SHE WAS ONCE.

Yes, but she didn't have any brothers. She only had

a sister, Margaret, who was younger than her.

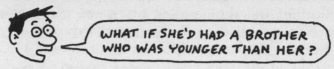

He would have become king.

Of course, but royals have been doing it this way for centuries.

So now you understand how succession works. What are your chances? Pretty slim, I'm afraid. Look at this family tree of the present royal family. What do you notice?

There are lots of them. Well spotted. Charlie is next in line for the throne after his mum, then come Charlie's sons, Prince William and Prince Harry, then Charlie's younger brother, Andrew, and then his children, Beatrice and Eugenie, and so on. Even if that lot were out the way there are still umpteen others including relatives you've never heard of like Prince Haakon Magnus of Norway...

So you see, succeeding to the throne is not going to be easy. Far quicker is...

2 Murder

I'LL SEND THEM MY HOMEWORK, THEY'LL DIE OF BOREDOM!

Killing your relatives so you can be king or queen is frowned upon these days. Yet at one time it was quite the fashion. If you're not the next in line and you're in a hurry, why not bump off anyone that's in your way?

Take Richard III. He was way down the list when it came to the succession. But all the people in front mysteriously died or came to nasty ends. Edward IV died, and left his sons Edward V and little Richard. Tricky Dicky suggested they'd be more comfortable in the Tower of London where they mysteriously (surprise, surprise) died. Richard III claimed the throne and no one has ever been able to pin the murders on him for sure.

In case you're thinking no one would miss a few royals, there are two things you should consider. Firstly, the Queen has a long line of relatives who would succeed to the throne before you. By the time you'd bumped them all off you'd probably be dead yourself.

Secondly, plotting to murder the sovereign is known as treason. At one time anyone found guilty of treason was executed. These days you might keep your head but spend a lifetime at Her Majesty's Pleasure. That doesn't mean waiting on the Queen!

3 Marriage

Marriage is a tried and tested passport to becoming a royal. According to fairy tales if a princess kisses a frog it will turn into a handsome prince and they'll get married. Sadly this story isn't much help unless you happen to be a frog.

However, you can marry a royal prince or princess without having webbed feet. How do you go about this? First you have to meet them. Spoilt royals often turn up unexpectedly. So it's just a matter of hanging about in the right place. Here's a handy step-by-step guide to meeting your royal match.

Make a royal match

1 See the "what's on" guide in the paper.

2 Get in any way you can.

3 Wait in line to meet the royal of your dreams.

4 Say something original.

5 Present her with a bunch of flowers

6 Offer to take her home afterwards.

Marrying a royal may not be so easy. And there's another small problem. Modern royals don't have a very good record on marriage. Three of Liz's four children have married. All three also got divorced. Liz's sister, Margaret, split from her hubby too. And Princess Anne is on to her second. So much for living happily ever after. So succession, murder and marriage don't look promising. That leaves...

4 Monopoly

Looking royal

So you see it *is* possible to become a spoilt royal. But if you succeed there will be lots to learn. Some people have become royals only to be told they're not behaving ... well, *royal* enough. Take Fergie (the Duchess of York). She was very popular when she first married Prince Andrew. People said she was a breath of fresh air. But her popularity soon took a nosedive. Although her dad was a Major, Fergie was always out of step.

The papers grumbled that she was too fat, too loud, and left her kids with nannies while she went dashing off round the world. They also called her Freebie Fergie because she kept accepting expensive presents.

Maybe her real crime was that she didn't behave like a real royal. Royals have certain ways of doing things. They sit, stand and even walk differently from the rest of us.

It is easy to spot the royal species. The diagram on the next page will help you. Look in a mirror to check how you compare ...

The royal species

EARS
STICK OUT LIKE
ROYAL MUG HANDLES

NOBLE BROW

ROMAN NOSE
PASSED DOWN FROM
ROMAN EMPERORS

REGAL SMILE

BLUE BLOOD
(RED IS SUCH A
COMMON COLOUR)

HANDS
HELD BEHIND BACK,
PREVENTS NOSE
PICKING IN PUBLIC

BOW LEGS
FROM HOURS
SPENT ON
HORSEBACK

CLOTHES
TWEEDY

FEET
PLANTED SQUARELY
TO AVOID FALLING
OVER IN PUBLIC

How to wave like a royal

1 Bend arm at elbow.
2 Hold hand upright.
3 Rotate hand stiffly
in a circle.
4 Try to smile and nod
at the same time.
Note: Normal waving is
tiring and doesn't give
the right impression.

How to speak royal

And it doesn't stop there. Not only will you need to look royal, you'll need to speak the Queen's English. This is not as easy as it sounds. It's not just a matter of treating everyone as if they're your unpaid servants (although that's a good start). Royals have their own coded language. The Queen for example uses the royal "We" a lot. She isn't talking about the luxury loos at Buck House. When the Queen says "we" she means herself – as in ...

WE ARE NOT AMUSED.

She talks about herself as if she is two people. Bonkers? Yes, but spoilt royals can act any way they like. So what if she actually does need a royal wee? She will probably say ...

PRAY EXCUSE US, WE NEED TO ATTEND TO URGENT MATTERS OF STATE

ZOOM!

Learning to talk royal takes some practice. There are lots of strange words and funny ways of saying them. Royals generally speak as if their mouths are stuck together with chewing gum.

Our royal dictionary will clue you in on useful royal words.

To help you pronounce them the royal way, try saying each word as it's written in brackets.

19

A royal dictionary

The Commonwealth (The Caw-man-wealth)
One of the Queen's many titles is Head of the Commonwealth. The Commonwealth was dreamed up in 1926. Someone once explained it as an old boys' club for ex-members of the British Empire. (In 1990 a quarter of the world's people belonged. It was a big empire.) Countries like Australia and Canada have left the Empire but still regard Elizabeth as their queen.

Corgis (caw-gies, dah-lings, didd-ums)
The royals have always been dog lovers. The Queen is especially fond of Welsh corgis. She was first given one in 1944 and called it Susan. Soon after, Princess Margaret, in a fit of jealousy, picked up Susan and threw her in a lake. Having second thoughts, Margaret then jumped in herself, fully clothed and rescued the dog. Susan was only a little damp and went on to be spoilt rotten like all royal pets.

The Queen feeds the corgis herself. She dishes out chopped liver and dog biscuits every day with a silver fork and spoon. In the early days of her reign, Liz wore her heavy crown on her head to feed the dogs. She was learning how to balance it on her head (the crown not the corgis).

Curtsy (curt-say)

Boys have to bow before the Queen, girls are expected to curtsy. Even spoilt princes and princesses have to bow or curtsy before foreign royals. They practise from an early age. The Queen learnt to curtsy before she was two. But now she's Queen she doesn't curtsy to anyone.

If you've never learnt this useful skill don't worry. Here's how to do it:

1 Plant left leg behind right leg.

2 Sink gracefully towards the floor like a dying swan.

3 Hold out dress as if saying, "Isn't this nice material?"

4 Rise back to standing and wait for marks out of ten.

Note: Jeans are not suitable for curtsies as they make a nasty ripping sound.

MORE LIKE A DEAD DUCK THAN A DYING SWAN!

God Save the Queen! (Gawd Sev the Quin)

This is what you shout whenever the Queen is passing by. It's also the lyrics of her signature tune, known as the national anthem.

Nobody knows who wrote *God Save the Queen* (or king). The song dates back at least to 1745. It was performed at the Theatre Royal, Drury Lane, in

London on 28 September 1745 for King George II. It was instantly a big hit. It would have soared to number one in the charts if only they'd had Radio 1. Within a few years the anthem was being played every time the King made an appearance in public.

Don't forget you're meant to stand up whenever you sing the Queen's song.

This is a cunning trick to make sure she gets a good seat.

Gordonstoun (Gawd-on-stun)
The name of a posh school in Scotland where royals are sent. Prince Philip went there. So did his sons Charles and Andrew. While he was head boy, Andrew was known to his schoolchums as "the great I am" (were they hinting he was spoilt?).

Investiture (Investi-chewer)
The ceremony when the Queen hands out honours to her subjects. People like Cliff Richard and Paul McCartney are made knights. At one time knights used to clank around in suits of armour. Sadly they don't have to do that any more. A knighthood just means you can call yourself Sir Cliff or Sir Paul.

Polo (peau-low)

If a royal asks, "Do you like polo?" it doesn't mean, "Fancy a mint?" Polo is the strange sport where you ride a horse and belt a ball with a long-handled mallet. Charles's polo team used to be called "Young England". But once all the players got old and wrinkly they thought the name was a bit out-of-date.

WE CAN'T CALL OURSELVES 'OLD ENGLISH' — WE'LL SOUND LIKE MARMALADE!

Rifts (rifts – easy eh?)

In our family we do not have rifts. A very occasional row but never a rift

Princess Margaret

A tiff is a polite royal word for a row or argument. Of course rows between members of the royal family never happen. Or that's the story they want us to believe. Rumour says that some spoilt royals can't stand the sight of each other. For example, it's said that Charles never liked his brother-in-law, Mark Philips. Charles is supposed to have nicknamed him Foggy. Why? Because he was thick and wet!

Even the Queen is said to be capable of family feuding. Princess Michael once said on TV that she

23

thought the royal corgis should be shot! It's easy to imagine what the Queen thought of that.

Your Majesty (Yaw Maj-er-stee)
Never speak to the Queen until spoken to. Then you must address her "Yaw Majerstee". After that you can call her "Ma'am", which rhymes with *jam*. If you keep on saying "How are you, Your Majesty? Isn't it warm, Your Majesty? Who do you fancy at the races, your Majesty?" she may start tapping her foot. This is a sure sign that Her Majesty is getting annoyed.

Walkabout (warkabite) When royals go for a stroll amongst their subjects it's called a walkabout. The Queen first did this in New Zealand in 1970 walking a record 400 yards while hob-nobbing with members of the public. When members of the royal family go walkabout, people appear from nowhere and rush to get close to them. They are not devoted fans, they are the royals' personal bodyguards.

COULD YOU GUARD A LITTLE LESS PLEASE — ONE CAN'T BREATHE!

MEET THE FAMILY

I'm very lucky because I have very wise and incredibly considerate parents who have created a marvellous, secure happy home.

Prince Charles

AND THEY'RE FABULOUSLY RICH, TOO!

So you've made it. By fair means or foul you've become a spoilt royal. Goodbye homework, fish fingers and tidying your own bedroom. Hello champagne, silk knickers and servants.

I CAN STAY IN BED ALL DAY WATCHING T.V.

Sorry, it's time for breakfast. And the first thing you'll notice is that you've acquired a new family. And *what* a family! Royals are fond of saying they're just like any other people. This is a whopping great fib. Of course they're different. They're rich, pampered and spoilt rotten! They travel by private jet and yacht. They hobnob with presidents, film stars and aristocrats. They even look royal. Put them in a flat cap and they still wouldn't look right in Coronation Street. It's something to do with breeding.

Here's a portrait of your new family. Take a good look at them.

This isn't all of them of course. We couldn't get them all in the picture. As a royal you'll have a vast army of spoilt relatives – all with crackpot titles. You'd better get to know them. Royals prefer not to be called "love" or "matie". Liz, Charlie or "Eddie babe" won't go down well either. Learn their correct titles. There are lots of them. One name isn't enough for royals, they like to be spoilt for choice.

The top ten royals (and their titles)

1 The Queen – also known as HRH the Queen. All royals have the letters HRH in front of their name. It means Her (or his) Royal Highness. You may also call her Elizabeth II – except in the Isle of Man where she's the Lord of Man. (I know she's a woman but what can you expect from an island with three legs on its flag?)

2 HRH Prince Philip – the Queen's husband. Also known as the Duke of Edinburgh. The inhabitants of Papua New Guinea prefer to call him: Number-one-fellah-belong-Missus-Queen. This is about right but don't try it yourself, he's got a bit of a temper.

3 HRH Prince Charles. The Queen's eldest son and heir to the throne. Also called the Prince of Wales. You would think this would mean he lives in Wales. But it doesn't. Royal titles seldom make sense.

4 HRH Prince William of Wales. Charles's eldest son. Never borrow his bike without asking, he'll be King William in the future. His younger brother is...

5 HRH Prince Henry, but you may call him Harry. Confusing isn't it?

6 HRH Prince Andrew. The Queen's second son. Other titles: the Duke of York, Soya Hun (the name given to him by the Algonquin Indians. It means heir of the Earth).

7 HRH Prince Edward. Charles and Andrew's kid brother – but he's grown up so don't call him "kiddo".

8 HRH Princess Anne. You may also call her the Princess Royal.

9 HRH Princess Margaret, the Queen's younger sister. Also called Countess of Snowdon.

10 HRH The Queen Mother, also known as the Queen Mum. This is bad English but royals never worry about things like that.

Pass the sugar, fishface

So that's your new family. I told you there were a lot of them. And we haven't yet mentioned Fergie (not an HRH since she split from Andy). Then there's the endless list of uncles and aunts with odd names like Princess Michael of Kent (a woman, in case you're wondering).

Of course, no matter how spoilt your relatives are, it's difficult to say...

> PASS THE SUGAR, PLEASE, HIS ROYAL HIGHNESS, THE PRINCE OF WALES, THE DUKE OF CORNWALL, EARL OF... OH, FORGET IT.

What you need is a quick way of addressing a spoilt royal that won't offend them. Like most families, the royals have their own nicknames for each other. Here are some you could try.

Royal nicknames

Can you match the right nickname to the right royal?

1 Philip in his Glory   **a)** The Queen
2 Fishface   **b)** Charles
3 Lilibet   **c)** Princess Margaret
4 Charley's Aunt   **d)** Prince Philip
5 Piggyface

Answers: Well spotted – there are five nicknames but only four royals. The Queen has two nicknames because she's even more spoilt than the rest. **1d)** Nickname for Prince Philip invented by his European relations. **2b)** Princess Diana's nickname for Prince Charles when they were married. **3a)** The royal family's pet name for the Queen. **4c)** The name Princess Margaret gave herself after Charles was born. **5a)** The Queen again – a nickname her family use when she's in a bad mood.

29

Growing up

Life with the royal family is never dull. There's always a new country to visit, a hospital to open or a big royal bash just around the corner.

It may all seem a bit bewildering at first. Royals always act as if they know exactly what they're doing. They are trained to do this from an early age. From the moment they can suck on a silver spoon they are learning how to behave like a spoilt royal.

Born to be spoilt

When monarchs give birth it's a fairly private affair nowadays. Just the Queen and her private doctor. It wasn't always so. Up until 1936, members of Parliament were present at every royal birth to witness the great event!

The baby in the warming pan

This strange tradition started in 1688 when King James II was on the throne. James and his queen, Mary, weren't popular with everyone. They were Catholics and the Protestants wanted to get rid of them. They dreaded the birth of a royal prince. That would mean the Catholics kept their hands – and bottoms – on the English throne. So when Mary became pregnant, the Protestants did their best to cast doubt on the birth…

1
1687
QUEEN MARY BECOMES PREGNANT

TOO MANY POTATOES, DEAR?

2
RUMOURS SPREAD THAT THE QUEEN HAD INVENTED THE PREGNANCY

IT'S ONLY A CUSHION, YOU KNOW

3
20 JUNE 1687
THE QUEEN GIVES BIRTH

PHEW IT'S COLD, FETCH A WARMING PAN

4
A HEALTHY BOY IS BORN, SADLY NONE OF THE GOVERNMENT ARE THERE TO SEE HIM

THEY CAN'T STAND THE SMELL OF NAPPIES!

The result of all this daft behaviour was that parliament got upset. They insisted that in future the Home Secretary should witness all royal births. This practice went on until 1930. When the Queen's sister, Princess Margaret, was born in Glamis Castle there were two witnesses. They were Labour's Home Secretary, Jim Clynes and a Mr Boyd from the Home Office. As far as we know, neither of them called for a warming pan.

Name that child

As we've seen, names are important to spoilt royals. Princes can't be called names like any Charles, Will or Harry. Their parents have to choose something dignified and royal sounding.

WHAT ABOUT PRINCE DAN?

Just doesn't sound right does it?
Royals take great pains to choose the right name.

Possible Names

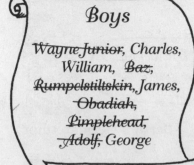

Boys	Girls
~~Wayne Junior~~, Charles, William, ~~Baz~~, ~~Rumpelstiltskin~~, James, ~~Obadiah~~, ~~Pimplehead~~, ~~Adolf~~, George	Elizabeth, ~~Cinderella~~ Beatrice, ~~Flopsy~~, Victoria, ~~Mrs Tiggywinkle~~, ~~Bimbo~~, ~~Jezebel~~, ~~Boopsy~~, Margaret, ~~Peaches~~

School for royals

As soon as a royal baby is born it has to be carefully spoilt. Ordinary schools are hopeless for this important task. Most kings and queens of England felt that school was best avoided all together. (You probably agree with them.) Schools are generally filled with commoners. They are cold, dirty, noisy places, sadly lacking in servants to do your work for you. Certainly no place for a royal to be spoilt in the correct manner.

This didn't mean that royal children were left to roam the palace free, firing catapults at the butler. Until recently royals were educated at home. Their teachers were anyone their parents dragged in to do the job. Not surprisingly, lessons weren't always successful. (Imagine what could happen if *your* parents chose a teacher for you!) Royals had never been to school so they had no idea what a good teacher looked like. Their choices were usually hopeless.

Royals and their teachers
1 Poor Bertie

> *It isn't only that he is inattentive, but when I scold him he just pulls my beard.*

Bertie's German tutor

Queen Victoria's son Bertie (later Edward VII) knew how dotty a royal education could be. The point of Bertie's schooling was to make him just like his German father Albert, a proud, clever and disciplined man. Bertie's schooling was based on a strict timetable drawn up by the fierce Baron Stockmar. The Baron had educated Albert. He believed in six-and-a-half hours of lessons a day – and no breaks for playtime.

Bertie's tutors tried to cram as many facts as possible into his poor brain. Sadly there wasn't much room in there!

The prince was never allowed to play games or mix with boys of his own age. Girls were completely forbidden (which explains why Bertie spent the rest of his life chasing after them). In order to liven up his lessons, Bertie took to making faces, spitting and throwing stones at his teacher. Once, while out on a walking tour, he drove a flock of sheep into Lake Windermere.

In the end, Bertie's education achieved exactly the opposite of what his mum had intended. Instead of turning out like his father, Bertie couldn't have been more different. Albert was tall, slim and clever, he never smoked, drank or chased girls. Bertie in comparison was short, fat and foolish. He smoked large cigars, drank like a fish and wanted to kiss every woman he met! Maybe things didn't turn out so bad – he was a true spoilt royal!

2 Crawfie and the Queen

The Queen and her sister, Princess Margaret, were taught to read by their mother. Later a nursery governess called Marion Crawford was put in charge of lessons. "Crawfie" had strict instructions on what was fitting for young princesses. They were to be outdoors a great deal, to "acquire good manners and perfect deportment and to cultivate the feminine graces". Translated, that meant they were to act like young ladies. Belching contests were strictly out.

Crawfie didn't always find it easy teaching her royal pupils. Once, when the young Queen behaved badly, her governess refused to speak to her. After a tense silence the Queen shouted …

YOU MUST ANSWER. IT'S ROYALTY SPEAKING!

Crawfie later got her own back. She left royal service and published a book spilling the beans on her time at the palace. The royals were not amused.

3 A charlie at school

By the time Charles and Anne were born, royal views had changed. Maybe the Queen didn't want to risk another Crawfie in the palace or perhaps she fancied a bit of peace and quiet. Whatever the reason, her children became the first royals in history to go to school. She packed their egg sandwiches and sent them off to catch the bus to the local primary.

THAT'S ONE'S PACKED LUNCH

Actually it wasn't quite like that. Prince Charles followed in his father's footsteps to school. (They were worried he might get lost on the way.) The Queen said Charles needed "as normal an upbringing as possible". So they sent him hundreds of miles away to an expensive Scottish public school called Gordonstoun. Charles hated it so much he described it as a "prison sentence". The school set out to "make a man" of boys by tough discipline. That meant long cross-country runs and cold showers. Charles wasn't the he-man type like his dad and he was bullied mercilessly. His class mates made fun of him and called him "Jug Ears". On the sports field he came off worst in rugby matches. Bullies queued up to land a punch on the future king of England. Not surprisingly his letters home were full of misery. He once complained, "I don't like it much here. I simply dread going to bed as I get hit all night long".

Wouldn't it be interesting to sneak a look at Charles' school report? Luckily, I happen to have it right here.

Which of the following teachers' reports about Charles are true?

Royal School Report

Name: Charles Windsor. Prince of Wales.

Class: 4B.

Class teacher: Mr Grovel OBE.

Mathematics: Hopeless. It will take a miracle for him to pass his exams.

Music: Painful. He has taken up the trumpet. I've advised him to put it down again quickly.

Physical Education: Hopeless. Captain of the first eleven football. Lost every game this season. Goals for: 4, Goals against: 82.

Religious Education: Shocking! He threw the Moderator of the Church of Scotland into a fountain.

Drama: Promising. Starred as Macbeth in school play. A natural at making long, boring speeches.

Art: Dismal. Insists on painting self-portraits. Says no other subject is as interesting.

History: Tiresome. Can recite the Kings and Queens of England — and does so every lesson!

English: Vile. Has learned some new words this term. Most of them unrepeatable.

Form teacher's comments: He should make an excellent Head Boy.

Goodbye schooldays

By the time you're old enough to leave school, you should be well and truly spoilt. You are ready to join the rest of the family and enter the wonderful world of royal work.

WORK? I DON'T HAVE TO WORK DO I?

Of course you do. There are banquets to attend, concerts to sit through, yachts to sail, polo matches to win, far away places to visit, expensive clothes to wear and more titles to accept. Step this way – and don't forget to wipe your feet on the red carpet...

SNOOTY DUTIES

And so to work. What exactly are royals meant to do?

SUNBATHE BY THE POOL ALL DAY? COUNT THE CROWN JEWELS?

Sorry, even spoilt royals have duties to attend to.

Here's what the Queen's grandad, King George V, did on a typical day.

A (boring) day in the life of King George V

Wake up at seven. Wash, trim beard and apply lavender water.
Dress smartly in suit or uniform.
Go downstairs, tap the barometer.
Work on state papers, write up my diary (doze off briefly).
Read The Times, sit down to breakfast on stroke of nine.

SNIP SNIP

YAWN

TICK TOCK
TICK TOCK TICK

SIGH...

Receive ministers, ambassadors and so forth –
(try not to doze off).

Take my daily stroll – exactly one mile around
the Palace garden.
Lunch with Queen at 1.30 pm sharp.
After lunch doze off in armchair for 15 minutes.
Then afternoon engagements and a thrilling
hour with my stamp collection.
ZZZZZZZZ...doze off again, writing out
what I do all day.

BORING OR WHAT? I WANT TO LIVE IT UP!

Luckily royals these days aren't half so dull. The Queen and her family are always out and about at royal bashes. There's plenty of food and drink and famous people falling over themselves to meet you. And if things do get a bit dull, a royal scandal in the newspapers will soon hot things up.

The Queen herself has kept a daily diary since she was a girl. It's in the leather bound volumes she keeps by her bedside. One of the early volumes is on display to the public. It's open at the page of her parents' coronation day.

But wouldn't you rather peek at a more recent entry?

41

A day in one's life

7.30 a.m. Woken by maid bringing in the tea (my special blend made by R. Twining and Company of the Strand, London). One takes tea with milk and no sugar as one is always reminding the maid. (The girl has a brain like a tea-bag – full of little holes.)

Can hear Philip down the corridor, coughing and slurping his coffee like a tramp. Thank goodness one doesn't have to share a room with him. Go downstairs in one's dressing gown to feed corgis (the little poppets!).

Must give cook one's instructions for tonight's dinner. The King of Norway is dropping in. What on earth do Norwegians like to eat? Herring?

8.15 a.m. Breakfast with Philip. Toast and coffee (from the Savoy Hotel Coffee Department). Philip remarks that one is looking splendid today. At least he may have said that. One has to guess at his growls from behind the paper.

9.30 a.m. Press officer arrives with cuttings from the morning newspapers. Damn and blast! More stories about Fergie. Thought we'd got rid of her but no such luck.

10.00 a.m. Do one's paperwork. More government bills to sign. Philip had spilt coffee over one (not me, the bill), so chucked it in the bin. Don't suppose anyone will miss one less law. Already got far too many in one's humble opinion.

11.00 a.m. *Read a few of one's letters – 24 begging letters, 17 invitations to open airport toilets and one gift of a smelly haggis from a mad woman in Aberdeen.*

The usual stuff. Gave haggis to corgis. They ate it and were sick.

2.00 p.m. *Went to the races at Ascot. Goodie! One's horse came in at 50-1. Philip and I had to disguise ourselves as commoners to collect our winnings. Frightfully good fun. Philip nearly gave the game away by winking at passers by and shouting, "Wotcher mate!"*

4.00 p.m. *Open new hospital in the afternoon. Lots of sick people. Keep at a safe distance to wave and smile.*

7.00 p.m. *Dinner with King of Norway. Herring ghastly. King suggests one sends out for pizza. Never had pizza before. Rather yummy if one can get it on one's fork.*

9.00 p.m. *At last! Chance to take off one's crown and relax in front of the TV. Not even a mention of one on the Nine O'clock News. Humph!*

11.00 p.m. *Palace gates are closed. Dogs patrolling the grounds. Rather nice policeman on duty outside my bedroom. All as it should be. Now I can get back to my important reading.*

Dates for your diary

Royals hate routine. Who wants to do the same thing every day? (apart from George V of course). Certainly not spoilt royals. They like change and variety. During the year they keep moving between five different homes. They throw state banquets for visiting royals (lots of talking and eating food). Then the Queen and her family visit other countries (lots of talking and eating foreign food).

Some duties turn up every year though. Here are a few important dates for your diary.

Snooty duty 1: The trooping of the colour (June)

This ceremony marks the Queen's official birthday. Being a spoilt royal, the Queen has two birthdays instead of one. That way she gets more presents. Her real birthday falls on 21 April. Her official one is in June when it's less likely to pour with rain.

The Queen's official birthday is always marked at the Horse Guards parade in London. The Queen's job is to inspect the troops of the Household Division in their bearskins.

No, not *bare* skins. Bearskins are the black busby hats that they wear. In the past soldiers looked to the regimental flag to know their position in battle. If they couldn't recognize the flag they were in big trouble, so it was trooped in front of them before the fight began. Colours haven't actually been sent into battle since the Crimean War, so it's all pretty pointless, but it looks very nice and thousands of tourists turn out to watch it.

Q Why does the clock at the parade ground have to be adjusted each year?

A To make sure it strikes eleven exactly as the Queen makes her entrance.

Snooty duty 2: Garden parties (June)

Most garden parties mean a few deckchairs on the lawn and waiting for the barbecue to heat up. A royal garden party is different. The Queen gives three a year at Buckingham Palace and one at Holyrood Palace in Scotland. Instead of a few friends she invites a football crowd. Up to 10,000 people arrive wearing their best party clothes.

At 4 p.m. exactly the Queen and her family appear on the terrace. They all take a different route, stopping to talk to guests on the way. The Queen is well practised at cutting people off if they're talking too much. She just takes a step away from them, flashes her best smile and is gone.

Afterwards tea is taken in the royal tent. On the menu are dainty cucumber sandwiches, chocolate cake, ice-cream and of course endless cups of tea. Visitors may be disappointed to find the teaspoons are just ordinary stainless steel. The Queen did once use her own collection of teaspoons with the royal crest. At the end of the day 1,000 of them got pinched!

Snooty duty 3: The changing of the guard (every day – April–September)

Strictly speaking you won't have to take part in this. But since it takes place in your front yard, you should know about it. It's always fun to pull back the curtains and goggle with the tourists.

The sentries outside Buckingham Palace in their red jackets and black busbies belong to five different regiments – the Grenadiers, the Coldstream Guards, the Welsh, Scots and Irish Guards. The only way to tell them apart is the colour of their plumes and the number of their buttons. Getting too close to count their buttons can be dangerous however, especially if you're a tourist. When the guard changes there is lots of marching up and down, stamping and thumping of rifle butts.

This is done as a warning to the army of watching tourists. You may not know it, but the palace guards and the tourists are at war.

The War of Buckingham Palace

Sentries are changed every two hours outside the palace. They have a code of hand signals to help them to communicate without speaking.

Snooty duty 4: The Queen's speech – Christmas Day

It was King George V who first had the bright idea of a Christmas broadcast to the nation. He made his first broadcast on radio in 1932 (people didn't have tellies then). George VI probably cursed his Dad's brilliant idea. He had a bad stammer and worried that his speech might be the longest ever on radio.

Today the text of the Queen's speech is always kept top secret. (Even though she never says anything juicy.) In 1992 *The Sun* newspaper caused an uproar by printing the speech two days before it came out at Christmas.

The Queen was said to be hopping mad. The press had ruined her Christmas and there was even talk of the Palace taking the newspaper to court. It all ended with *The Sun* offering a cheeky apology the next day and offering to pay £200,000 to charity.

Barmy customs

As well as garden parties, speeches and parades, there are lots of ceremonies connected with royalty. Some of them are downright weird. Which of the following actually happen?

1 The Trial of the Pyx

Each year a jury of goldsmiths get together in Goldsmiths Hall. The Queen's Remembrancer is head of the jury and tries to remember to be there.

And who is on trial? A handful of coins. No, really. The jury's job is to make sure that the coins are the right size and weight.

2 Come out wherever you are!

Ever since Guy Fawkes's plot to blow up Parliament, the cellars and corridors of Westminster are searched every year. The search takes place before the Opening of Parliament. The Yeomen of the Guard poke around the cellars with lanterns. These days the police tag along too with torches and sniffer dogs.

3 Swan upping

Swans are often given marks to show who they belong to. There is an ancient custom that all mute swans that are unmarked belong to the Queen. So every year people called Dyers and Vintners go round marking swans. Why? Just in case the Queen tries to pinch them of course!

WATCH OUT - SHE'LL STOP AT NOTHING

4 Presenting the Leeks

On 1 March the regiment of the Welsh Guards take a leek. This doesn't mean they all go to the loo at once. The leeks in this case are vegetables and an important Welsh national symbol. A member of the royal family presents leeks to the regiment because 1 March is St David's day. No one knows what the soldiers do with the leeks – maybe they club together later and have a sneaky leeky soup?

5 Windsor soup

Have you heard of Windsor soup? Did you know it was the Queen who invented it? The Queen, always keen to save money, told her cooks to make any left over veg into soup. The result was brown Windsor soup. Ever since then the staff at Buck Palace have been given Windsor soup on Christmas day. The Queen herself never touches the stuff. She sticks to turkey with all the trimmings!

6 Royal Maundy

The older she gets the more money the Queen has to give to pensioners. On Maundy Thursday (Thursday before Easter Sunday), the Queen hands out special silver coins to twice as many elderly people as her own age. The Queen always carries a posy of flowers called a nosegay. This dates from the time of the Great Plague. The flowers are supposed to offer protection against plaguey pensioners.

> **Answer: 5** – The Queen didn't invent Windsor soup and luckily it's not made from Her Majesty's cast-off vegetables.

"Dear Queenie"

The Queen gets over 100,000 letters a year. That's a lot of letters. She has her own post office in the basement of Buck Palace to deal with it all. First, each letter and parcel has to be checked to make sure that it hasn't got a bomb inside. (Ticking parcels are handled very carefully.) Then the letters are sorted into different piles. Friends who write to the Queen have a secret code to show who they are.

They put their initials in the bottom left hand corner. Their letters then get passed to the Queen unopened. (So now you know the trick.) Official letters go to a government department. Routine stuff is answered by a private secretary without bothering the Queen. What about letters from children? They're answered by a lady-in-waiting. Sadly you can't get a personal reply from the Queen on the colour of the royal knickers.

The Queen does pick out a few letters each day and reads them herself. Her staff say she has developed an instinct for picking the most interesting ones.

She gets all kind of letters. Some want a spoilt royal to pay them a visit, some are begging for cash, and some want the Queen's help with a good cause. Then there is the royal fan club who write just for the thrill of getting a reply on Buckingham Palace notepaper. Finally letters come from people who are stark, staring bonkers and want the Queen to knight their pet budgie.

You might like to compose a letter to the Queen yourself. Here's one that arrived at the palace recently.

Dear Queenie,

   I know you're a busy person (me too, you should see the piles of homework I've got) so I'll come straight to the point. I think you should adopt me.

   I'm fed up with my own mum and dad. They're always sending me to bed when there's something good on TELLY. Also they are very stingy with pocket money. I'm sure you could spare more than a few MEASLY quid a week.

   I've seen you a lot on TV. You're not all that wrinkly for someone who's older than Windsor castle. I think you'd make a good mum. You could do with being a bit more TRENDY but I could help with that. (I'm sure you'll get to like my music after a while.)

   Don't worry. I won't mind moving to London. It's got lots of shops, cinemas and BURGER bars. (I like chips best, do you? I think it's important if you're going to cook for me.)

   Anyway think about it. I'm sending a picture of myself

   Write back soon. Or send round one of your coaches and I'll throw some clothes in my rucksack.
                    Yours adorably,
                              Dan xx

P.S. If you feel too OLD to adopt another son you could just send me a crown and lots of jewels. That would be OK with me.

Sporting royals

Not all royal duties are snooty. Part of the job of being a spoilt royal is to show your face in public. What better way to do it than by going to Royal Ascot, the F.A. Cup final or Wimbledon tennis championship? There are thousands of people there to see the royals. And it just so happens that they *love* sport. They're only doing their duty after all!

There are plenty of sporty events where you can see royals. Sometimes they take part, sometimes they just go to watch. Either way, spoilt royals like to take centre stage.

Each of the royals have their own fave sports.

Sporting royals gallery
The Queen

The Queen is devoted to horse racing. As she once said, "If it were not for my Archbishop at Canterbury, I should be off to Longchamps (the Paris racecourse) every Sunday."

ONE WANTS TO GO TO THE RACES

IF YOU BET ON A SUNDAY I BET YOU WON'T GET TO HEAVEN!

The Queen owns lots of horses. Her first racehorse was called Monaveen. She bought it when she was a princess, going half shares with her mum. The Queen's racing colours are purple with scarlet sleeves, gold braid and a black cap with a gold tassel. But she looks rather silly dressed like that, so the jockey wears them instead.

Prince Philip

The Prince often has to tag along to Royal Ascot races even though he hates it. Sometimes he hides a radio in his top hat so that he can listen to the cricket score. Philip used to play polo like Charles, but when he grew too old he took up carriage driving. All you need for this sport is your own carriage and team of horses. (Have a look in the garage to see if you've got one.) Philip soon became an expert at carriage driving and has written a book on it. It's called *Competition Carriage Driving* (in case you want to get it out of the library).

Philip's other great love is shooting. Generally he shoots birds like grouse and pigeons. There are probably a few reporters he'd like to shoot too.

Prince Charles

When he was younger, Prince Charles fancied being a jockey. He could have been a success if he hadn't kept falling off his horse. His first race was at Sandown in 1980. The following year he came off with a bump on the same course. The papers gleefully showed pictures of the prince hitting the deck. Lots of reporters turned up for the prince's next race four days later. You can guess what they were hoping to see. And the prince didn't let them down. He fell off again. Soon after the prince wisely gave up racing and turned back to polo.

Princess Anne

Princess Anne used to be pretty nifty at something called three day eventing. (Royals don't go in for common sports like snooker or arm-wrestling.) A three day event is a kind of cross-country obstacle course for horses. It goes on for ages. Three days in fact. It's like show-jumping with muddy puddles. Smart alecs (like the press) wait at the water jump hoping to get a picture of a wet royal.

In 1976 Anne was picked to be part of Britain's event team at the Montreal Olympics. Female shot-putters at the time were getting so big and hairy that the judges wondered if they were really men. All women competitors were ordered to take a sex test. All except Princess Anne of course. No one was brave enough to ask her!

Boo for politics!

Of all snooty duties, the daftest are to do with politics.

Countries like Germany and America don't have spoilt royals, so the president is the top dog. In Britain we have the Queen as our Head of State, which means officially she's above the Prime Minister. Actually being Head of State doesn't add up to much. The Queen is a bit like a figurehead on a ship. The figurehead goes in front and looks impressive but the captain is the one in charge of the ship. The captain in Britain is the Prime Minister backed by his scurvy crew – the government. If they wanted Parliament could vote to do away with the Queen tomorrow. So far they haven't and because the Queen is Head of State every new law has to be passed with her permission.

WHAT IF SHE REFUSES TO PASS A LAW?

Good question. If she did, there might be a *constitutional crisis*.

M.P.s might start asking awkward questions like: "Who does the Queen think she is?" and "Who needs her anyway?" They might even end up voting to do away with the monarchy. The Queen doesn't want to risk that so she doesn't question what Parliament decides. Parliament goes on politely asking the Queen to sign laws. And the Queen goes on politely signing her autograph. It's a game where everyone agrees not to break the rules!

Pompous prime ministers

As if reading piles of papers isn't enough, the Queen actually has to meet her prime minister every week. It's enough to make any spoilt royal look for another job.

Spoilt royals of the past have often hated the sight of their prime ministers.

Here are a few things they've said about them.

He speaks to me as if I were a public meeting!

Queen Victoria on Gladstone

58

I would have as soon expected to see a pig in a church

King George IV on seeing Prime Minister
Robert Peel at Ascot races

Things have not got much better in modern times. Relations between the Queen and Mrs Thatcher (PM 1979-90) were said to be so cold the windows almost froze over.

When Mrs Thatcher had her first audience with the Queen things didn't start well. The Prime Minister was horrified to see they were wearing the same colour dress. Back home at Number 10, Mrs T contacted the Palace. In future, she wished to know in advance what the Queen would be wearing. There was no need, came the Palace's cool reply, "since Her Majesty doesn't notice what other people wear." Perhaps Mrs Thatcher should have gone in fancy dress. Then the Queen might have noticed her.

NICE HANDBAG, PRIME MINISTER

Open sez me

Another royal duty is to open parliament once a year. The State Opening of Parliament takes place in the autumn and the Queen does the honours personally. She likes all the royals to be there. If Philip comes, an extra throne has to be borrowed from the Marquess of Cholmondley, so Philip has somewhere to park his royal rear.

It's a real pantomime – with fairytale coaches, funny wigs, villains in black and things to shout out. It's the kind of spectacle that makes Britain what it is today. Barmy! Here's what happens...

1 The Queen travels to the Houses of Parliament in the Irish State Coach.

2 Meanwhile the state crown travels from the Tower of London, sitting on a velvet cushion in a carriage. Well, could *you* see a crown travelling by Number 42 bus?

3 The Queen arrives and goes to the Robing room where she gets into her costume. Her Robe of State is six metres long!

4 Wearing her State crown, the Queen makes her big entrance into the House of Lords to a fanfare of trumpets.

5 The Queen sits on her throne and sends a messenger to fetch the MPs from the House of Commons. (Don't forget she's not allowed in.)

6 The MPs crowd into the House of Lords to hear the Queen's speech. Actually they can't all get in. The ones that can, remain standing to show how mean and tough they are. Her Majesty then dons her royal specs and reads the Queen's speech. Of course it's not really *her* speech. The Government write it and they know what she's going to say anyway.

> MY GOVERNMENT WILL DO SOMETHING OR OTHER BLAH BLAH HO HUM YOU'RE NOT LISTENING ANYWAY ARE YOU NO, I CAN TELL I DON'T KNOW WHY I BOTHER I REALLY DON'T...

> ZZZ

Snooty duties can be a pain in the royal rump. But don't despair. If you grow tired of them you can always arrange a holiday somewhere nice. Just call it a state visit.

> I CALL IT A STATE VISIT BECAUSE I ALWAYS GO ON ONE WHEN I'M IN A BIT OF A STATE

ROYALS OF THE WORLD UNITE!

As part of the British royal family, you become a member of an exclusive group. Welcome to the World Royals Club. Admission at the door is strictly by flashing your crown or tiara.

YOU MEAN WE BRITS AREN'T THE ONLY ROYALS?

Not at all, they still have spoilt royals in Belgium, Bhutan, Holland, Sweden, Denmark, Morocco, Spain, Thailand, Tonga ... shall I go on?

Foreign visits

So what if you fancy dropping in on some of your royal pals? Nothing's easier. Just arrange a state visit. It's part of your royal duty to make stronger links between countries. And what better way to see the world than on a free trip paid for by the British taxpayer (that's the rest of us).

So where would you like to go?

DISNEYLAND! CLIMBING THE PYRAMIDS! SKIING IN THE ALPS!

Hold on a second. You haven't got the whole picture. When you arrive you'll have a whole list of engagements.

BRING ON THE PRINCESSES, I'LL GET ENGAGED TO THEM ALL!

Not that sort of engagement. You're more likely to watch parades, meet V.I.P.s and get shown round crumbly old buildings. As soon as you get off your royal jet a band will play the national anthem out of tune. Then lots of officials will queue up to shake hands with you. Next they'll ask you to inspect their troops. Before long you'll realize this is just what you left home to get away from!

When you're going on a state visit it pays to know the boy scout's motto: *be prepared*. The Queen must have been a boy scout at one time. She plans every trip as if she's backpacking across the Sahara Desert. You never know what you might need abroad. Her Majesty leaves nothing to chance and takes everything but the kitchen sink. On a trip to France in 1972 she took along her own gold cutlery and dinner service to throw a banquet for the French president. That time her luggage weighed almost a tonne. Three years later, on a trip to Mexico her stuff weighed a staggering six tonnes! (Of course it's her servants who do the staggering.) So start packing now. It may take a few days.

Odd one out

As well as bringing enough clothes for a fashion show, the Queen takes loads of other essential items on her travels. All the items pictured below are things the Queen takes with her on her royal visits — except for one! Which is it?

1. Feather Pillows
2. Hot Water Bottle
3. Favourite China Tea
4. Cases of Malvern Water
5. Barley Sugar for Travel Sickness
6. Electric Kettle with Royal Monogram
7. Special soft white loo seat to spoil Royal bottoms
8. Jewellery which has a special link to the country
9. Liz's contact lenses
10. Black edged writing paper just in case some cousin kicks the bucket
11. Camera

Of course even with the most careful planning things can go wrong sometimes. Like the time in Washington, U.S.A. where the royal staff were horrified to discover that they couldn't find the Queen's personal tea supply. She was reduced to making do with *tea bags* from the White House. Sometimes even royals have to suffer!

First class travel

So that takes care of the packing. How are you going to get there?

ER... BRITISH AIRWAYS?

Don't be vulgar, spoilt royals travel in style. No second class tickets for you. The royal family have their own personal fleet of transport. It's just a case of deciding how you want to travel.

The Queen's scrapbook

The Queen has visited countries all over the world – including every single member of the Commonwealth. She is given stacks of presents wherever she goes. Her palaces are chock-full with souvenirs. Some were so weird she had to stow them on the royal yacht – like a solid gold palm tree hung with ruby dates. (Who says money doesn't grow on trees?)

65

The Queen's scrapbook must be pretty impressive. Maybe you'd like to see a few pages? The facts are all true by the way (though we may have imagined the Queen's comments).

Travels with my tiara – The royal scrapbook

1953 *First state trip abroad – Commonwealth tour. Visited Bermuda, Jamaica, Panama, Fiji, Tonga, New Zealand, Australia – you name it, one went there. Made 102 speeches, shook 13,213 hands. If one hears God Save the Queen sung once more, one will strangle the singer personally. Brought back around 200 official presents. Shall keep most of them to give away on next trip. It's called royal recycling.*

1968 *Brazil. One never knows how awful the food will be when one is abroad. Safest to pack essentials oneself. Have brought emergency rations: three tins of Dundee cake, six packs of shortbread, eight boxes of "After Eight" mints, three bottles of mint sauce, three jars of raspberry jam, 36 bottles of champagne. That should get us through the weekend anyway.*

1979 Africa. One of the tribal chiefs cried out in astonishment, "My God the Queen is a woman!"

1979 Denmark. One visited Copenhagen's famous amusement park, Tivoli Gardens. Philip and I took a ride on the Tunnel of Love – in different boats of course. He went with the Queen of Denmark, I went in the other boat with her husband Prince Henrik. Tunnel of Love rather romantic. One likes to think it brought our two countries closer together.

1981 Norway. Encountered a spot of bother while inspecting the King's Guards. Rowdy I.R.A. supporters threw tomato ketchup at one. Luckily one was wearing bright red that day so doubt if anyone noticed.

67

1986 Visit to China. Wore red hat and coat, supposed to be Chinese lucky colour (especially if there's any ketchup flying around). Saw the Great Wall of China. More interested in the great tea in china (cups). Visit going swimmingly until Philip makes some remark about the Chinese having slitty eyes. Sometimes one wonders if he should be fitted with an enormous gobstopper.

1987 Andrew and Fergie's first state visit to Canada. Fergie complains that Canadian newspapers call her "Rowdy Fergie" and "Big Red".
Gifts received include a buffalo skull from an Indian tribe. Maybe Fergie could wear it and be known as "Big Red Buffalo". Just a suggestion.

1993 Australian visit. Australians are very relaxed and friendly. Especially the Prime Minister, Mr Paul Keating. It was a bit of a shock when one felt his arm round one's waist. Next he'll be asking one out to the pictures. Horrors! Just found out the man wants to make Australia a republic! That would mean they didn't need a Queen anymore. Next time he comes near one he'll get a swipe from one's handbag.

LET'S HAVE A BIG HAND FOR THE QUEEN!

NOT THERE YOU WON'T, MATEY!

Foul disasters

So much for the highlights of the last 40 years of royal travel. Of course everyone has their holiday disaster stories. Spoilt royals are no exception.

Quick royal quiz

Are the following foreign disasters true or false?

1 Anybody at home?

Once the Queen descended the plane steps in Dubrovnik (in former Yugoslavia) to be greeted by deafening silence.

The reception committee had rushed off to a place called Titograd. Someone had mistakenly told them that the Queen's flight had been diverted there. The Queen had to wait 20 minutes on her plane while a new reception committee was organized. There were plenty of red faces as the Queen shook hands.

2 Squashed topper

Visiting Australia, Princess Alexandra climbed into a limousine and sat down on the Governor's new silk top hat. Totally unabashed, she held it up to the crowd and shouted …

3 Cheeky welcome

The Queen hasn't always been welcomed by the Maoris, the native people of New Zealand. Maoris claim that Queen Victoria promised that they could keep their traditional lands and then broke her word. As Victoria's descendant, they hold the present Queen responsible. They threatened to greet her with a traditional Maori insult – baring their bottoms to her (a 21 bum salute!).

Several Maoris – men and women – managed to carry out their threat. The Queen, more used to smiling faces, pretended not to notice as they were dragged away.

4 Chilling out

Things can get pretty hot in Nigeria. So the Queen's thoughtful hosts put a refrigeration plant in her bedroom. It was supposed to lower the temperature of the room. And it worked – only too well. The floor had to be defrosted before the Queen could go in. Lucky Her Majesty takes her hot water bottle everywhere.

SHE'S DECIDED SHE LIKES IT FROZEN

5 So glad to be here

Making a speech in Canada, Prince Philip said, "The monarchy exists not for its own benefit, but for that of the country. We don't come here for our health. We can think of better ways of enjoying ourselves."

Funnily enough the Canadians were not very impressed. A few weeks later the Queen's head disappeared from some Canadian banknotes. It was replaced by some of the country's ex-Prime Ministers. Nice one, Philip!

6 Hats off

Just before the Queen visited Nigeria a rumour started in Lagos, the Capital. It said that you had to take off your hat when in the presence of royalty.

71

The Nigerians in their thousands all went out to buy hats so that they could take them off.

Answers Disaster! All of them are true!

Letter from Tonga

So your suitcase is packed, the plane is waiting and the servants are lined up to wave you off. Which royal will you visit first? What about the island of Tonga? You'll find the king there is twice the man of most royals.

Dear Liz,

You'd love it here. Tonga is like the island of your dreams. Palm trees, sandy beaches, and Royals are treated like GODS!

Went to visit the king in his wooden palace yesterday. He is called King Taufa'ahau Tupou IV. Tupou is big. Think of a sumo wrestler in dark glasses. He used to be 200 kilos, but he's on one of his diets at the moment. The king works out in a gym every day and rides a bicycle. (It has a special saddle designed to take the royal big bottom.)

Most Tongans are fatsos and proud of it. It's the eating that does it. A Tongan potato (called a yam) can be over two metres long! The king worries that his people are too fat. He's put scales in the banks so they can weigh themselves and see if they're getting slimmer. (They AREN'T.)

King Tupou is a music-lover. He loves to be woken by a BRASS BAND outside his window (maybe you should try this at Buck House?) Tupou himself plays the guitar and electric organ. While at Sandhurst (the

72

English college for army officers) he formed a band called the Straight Bananas.

Like I said, they know how to SPOIL royals here. When the king appears, Tongans all fall to the ground. The king has to have a private cabin if he travels by plane. Otherwise all his people get out of their seats and sit on the floor.

There's a lot you could learn from Tupou. Why put up with pesky POLITICIANS? The king solved the problem by making himself Prime Minister!

There is no limit to his talents (or his waistline). Who holds the national pole-vault record? Tupou. Who invented goalposts which can be used for both rugby and football? Tupou. Who created a new method of adding up in schools? (I'll give you a clue - it wasn't the teacher.)

You should really visit soon. Who knows what eating a few of those giant yams might do for you?

Yours, fat and happy,

Dan ×x

A royal selection box

When you're back from Tonga there are lots of other royals to visit. And these top bananas are a pretty strange bunch. Here are just a few you could drop in on.

1 King Hassan of Morocco

King Hassan is one of the few people who've dared to be rude to the Queen. On a state visit to Morocco in 1980, the Queen was kept waiting time and again. First Hassan failed to turn up for a lunch in the Queen's honour (he was playing golf). Then, when he met her at his palace, he rudely ordered her ladies-in-waiting to leave the room. (One was the Duchess of Grafton. The king obviously took her for a chamber maid.)

Next the Queen was left sitting in her car for half an hour. Hassan was deciding whether he would attend dinner. He didn't. The final straw was a picnic in the Moroccan desert. The Queen was kept waiting in a tent for more than half an hour while her host lounged in his air-conditioned caravan.

The Queen tapped her foot and her face was like thunder. It wasn't only the temperature that was at boiling point. Hassan managed to delay Her Royal Highness right to the very end. The Queen had to wait at the airport because Hassan suddenly decided he wanted to see her off. Back home the Queen sent him a message. "We have been especially touched by the way in which Your Majesty took such a *personal interest* in our programme."

Even royals can be sarky when they want to be.

(You may wish to skip Hassan on your tour, he probably won't turn up anyway.)

2 King Leka of Albania

Did you know there are two Prince Charleses living in Britain? The other one is Prince Charles Castroit de Renzi of Albania. He's an electricity clerk living in Stoke-on-Trent. In 1992, 47 years of harsh communism came to an end in Albania. Some Albanians think it's time to bring the king back. Prince Charles isn't interested though. Like his dad, Alfred, he thinks being king is a dangerous job. Wise Alf turned down the chance to topple King Zog of Albania in the 1930s. He said he would have to give up a decent job in the U.K.

A more likely claimant to the throne is son of Zog. (*Star Wars* has nothing on Albania!) Zog's son is Leka, a businessman living in South Africa until recently. In July 1997 Leka put on his battle dress, strapped a grenade and pistol to his belt, and marched through Tirana, the capital of Albania. A band of monarchists were at his side. Shots were fired. Leka, Son of Zog, declared, "I am the rightful king of the Albanians."

It's too early to say whether Darth Vader may challenge him.

3 King Mswati III of Swaziland

When Prince Charles visited Swaziland in 1987 he met the young King Mswati III. Mswati became king when he was only 17. He had been educated in England and chatted happily to Charles about their schooldays. The young king then introduced his mother. He used her full ceremonial title – the Great She Elephant. The mother elephant fastened some beads round Charles's neck. Then they watched some traditional dancing to a song specially written for the royal visit. Translated it meant, "Prince Charles why are you so confident? You don't even have a cow."

Exactly. The king's subjects believe he has magical powers. Mswati can make it rain, turn enemy bullets into water and even change himself into any animal. This might be a dangerous idea for our Queen. If she ever changed herself into a pheasant, Prince Philip might try to shoot her.

4 King Karl XVI Gustaf of Sweden

Note the dotty name. King Karl XVI Gustaf. In Sweden kings put the name of their dead daddy after their own. So our queen would be Queen Elizabeth II George – which sounds even more bonkers!

Gustaf is probably the least powerful king in Europe. He'd only just got settled on the throne when his government changed the laws. The king was no longer allowed to take part in government meetings. He couldn't appoint ministers or sign bills. Even worse, the Swedish parliament could give him the sack at any time. If they didn't think he was doing a good job they'd just say he'd abdicated. It's a bit like you saying to your teacher, "I think you're useless. You resign!"

OKAY. SHALL I STAND IN THE CORNER A WHILE FIRST?

Poor Gustaf is more of a cardboard king than a spoilt royal. About the only thing he can do is give out honours. Like the Brits, the Swedes love honours and have lots of them. But, unlike the Brits, the Swedes haven't got many royals left. Out of a population of six million there are only 600 noble families. And they aren't very spoilt either. Many of them live in crumbly castles without servants or central heating. Once a year they all get together for dinner in a medieval hall. You can imagine the conversation. They drone on about the old days – when kings were kings and ministers were sent to the chopping block.

5 Sultan of Yogyakarta
Some kings like to show off their importance by their names. The Sultan of Yogyakarta on the island of Java is one. His full name is Ngarso Dalem Sepayen-Dalem Ingkeng Sinuwen Kangjeng Sultan ... (sorry, it goes on like this for ages). What it

means is: Prostrate at his royal feet, the Most Noble Sultan, the One who Holds the Universe in his Lap, Commander-in-Chief, Servant of God the Merciful, Descendant of the Prophet, Regulator of Religion, Caliph of God, the Tenth on the throne in the Good Country of Yogyakarta, the Prosperous Abode of Rama.

Try getting *that* on a £10 note!

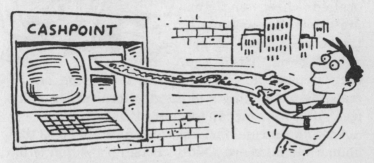

6 King Bhumibol Aiulyades of Thailand

King Bhumibol has gone one better than the Sultan of Yogyakarta. He is not just a servant of God, he *is* a god to many of his subjects. This can come in quite handy for a spoilt royal. You wouldn't want to argue with God, would you? (You might get struck by a lightning bolt.)

Most people in Thailand are Buddhists. Although the king was born in America and educated in Europe, he had to serve time as a simple monk in a Buddhist monastery like all males. Maybe this is what made Bhumibol into a wise king.

In Thailand governments change as often as the guards at Buck House. There have been 17 takeovers by the army since 1932! Luckily King Bhumibol is always on hand to sort things out.

It happened again in 1992. General Suchinda Krapray seized power and made himself Prime Minister. The General wasn't popular. There were mass protests in the streets and the army opened fire on the protesters. It seemed as if this time it had all got out of hand. Until the

king stepped in. Suchinda was later seen on TV crawling to the king and begging forgiveness at his feet. After all, you can't argue with God.

Another unusual fact about King Bhumibol is that he has one false eye. Oddly enough it led him to his wife. The story sounds like a fairytale but it's true.

When he was a young student Bhumibol liked to drive fast cars. One day he was in a serious accident and damaged his eyesight. The king was sent to Paris for an emergency operation. He didn't know whether he would ever see again. Before the operation his mother asked if there was anything he wanted. Bhumibol thought hard. "I would like to see the daughter of the Thai ambassador to France," he said. The ambassador's daughter was a schoolgirl called Princess Sirikit. The king had only met her once but she'd made a big impression.

Princess Sirikit came to visit the king in hospital. They fell in love and were married in 1950, a week before the coronation.

The operation was a success. So the king never lost sight of his lovely princess. And the Thai people don't seem to give a hoot that their god wears glasses.

7 Emperor Bokassa I of the Central African Republic

The Emperor was crowned in 1977. He wanted it to be a great event so he spent hours studying the video of Queen Elizabeth II's coronation. Every king and leader in Europe was invited. But, funnily enough, a lot of them found they were busy that day.

Bokassa saw himself as an African version of Napoleon, the famous French emperor-warrior. For the ceremony Bokassa wore a velvet tunic and shoes of pearl. His crown was an exact copy of Napoleon's with the French imperial eagle on the front. The Emperor sat on a gold throne next to the Empress Catherine. His golden coach was drawn by eight white horses brought

81

from Normandy, France. (Six other horses died in the terrible heat).

After the coronation 4,000 guests tucked into a French-style banquet. Musicians played soothing classical music. In one single day, Bokassa spent ONE THIRD of the entire country's wealth!

CRUMBLING OLD HEAPS

What with all those snooty duties and foreign visits, you might think that royals aren't spoilt at all.

MAYBE I SHOULD BE A LOO CLEANER, THEY GET TO SIT DOWN ON THE JOB.

Hang on, it's time to talk about the perks of the job. Royals, of course, don't live in ordinary houses like the rest of us. They live in a palace. And not just one palace; as usual, royals are spoilt for choice. They have dozens of crumbly castles, posh palaces and private houses where they can rest their heads. The Queen has so many homes, she probably keeps a calendar on the wall to remind her where she's living each month. It might look a bit like this.

Royal moving calendar

WHERE IS ONE TODAY?

January, February
Sandringham, Norfolk

Cancel milk, Pack Welly boots, headscarves, binoculars and bird-spotting book.

Easter
Windsor Castle

Pack Easter eggs, Crown, soda syphons - in case another nasty fire breaks out.

Early summer
Holyroodhouse, Scotland

Pack kilts, warm knickers, phrase book for understanding locals.

Autumn
Buckingham Palace, London

Cancel haggis. Pack bus pass, map of the underground, camera, check haven't left Philip or the Corgis in Scotland.

Christmas
Windsor Castle

Pack Christmas tree lights, baubles (crown jewels) one's speech for Christmas day, reading specs.

Dan's crumbly quiz

Since you'll be moving around a lot, it will help to know something about the royal digs. They are dotted all over England and Scotland. Most royal homes are great crumbly heaps that cost a fortune to keep up and take days to explore. Don't worry, you've got lots of time. If you keep moving house no one will know where you are half the time.

Just watch out for any lurking ghosts of dead royals – more about them later.

Can you answer a crumbly question about each royal heap?

1 Balmoral Castle

Where is it? In the middle of nowhere in Aberdeenshire, Scotland. The royals keep it as a summer hidey-hole where they can have

FORGET PHEASANTS, I'D RATHER SHOOT THE PRESS

picnics and shoot pheasants without the press poking their noses in.

Who owns it? The Queen.
She owns all the crumbly heaps, doesn't she? No, actually only Sandringham and Balmoral. The rest belong to the country.
House history? Bought by Queen Victoria and Prince Albert. They started the Ghillies Ball, an annual Scottish knees-up at the castle. The Queen and Prince wear tartan and dine to the wail of bagpipes.
What's inside? Wall to wall tartan.
Open to tourists? No thank you, the royals are on their hols. It's a private residence not a palace. So KEEP OUT or Prince Philip may fetch his gun.
Royal verdict: "The Highland Barn of 1,000 draughts." King Edward VII

Crumbly quiz question: Where did Queen Victoria get the money to buy Balmoral as her private home?
a) From selling royal treasures.
b) From Albert's piggy bank.
c) From the will of an eccentric miser.

---

2 Buckingham Palace
Where is it? You can't miss it. Bang in the middle of London – a short stroll down the Mall.

House history? The nickname "Buck house" isn't because the royals are making big bucks. The palace started as the London home of the Duke and Duchess of Buckingham. King George III made it a royal heap. He refused to live in St James's Palace – his Dad's old residence (they weren't good pals). George bought Buck House instead.

What's inside? More like a huge office than a home. But it does have a Chinese luncheon room (so the Queen and Philip can eat their Chinese take-away). It's also one of the few private homes to have its own nuclear fallout shelter.

Can we come in? Yes please. Millions of tourists part with their cash to see the Palace every year.

Royal verdict: "An icebox." – King George VI. "This isn't ours. It's a tied cottage." – Prince Philip.

Crumbly quiz question: King Edward VIII claimed the palace had a dank and musty smell. What's under Buck House that may explain the lingering pong?
a) A sewer.
b) A graveyard.
c) A family of skunks.

3 Clarence House

Where is it? Part of St James's Palace, London. The Queen Mum's place just down the road from Buck House. Close enough to drop in for a quick cuppa.

House history? Built in 1825–9 for William, Duke of Clarence (later William IV). Philip and Liz lived there after they got married but before she was Queen. When they moved in, the house was in such a state it didn't even have electricity. The royal newlyweds did it up and later handed it over to the Queen Mother.

What's inside? The Queen Mother of course.
Can we come in? Certainly not! She doesn't
want your dirty boots on her carpet.

Crumbly quiz question: Who traditionally
stays at Clarence House the night before a royal
wedding?
a) Royal brides.
b) The Archbishop of
Canterbury.
c) Anyone who'll pay
for bed and breakfast.

4 Holyrood House

Where is it? The Queen's gaff in Edinburgh,
Scotland.
House history? The holy bit dates from an
abbey founded there in 1128 by King David I.
The story goes that saintly King David was out
hunting when he should have been at his
prayers. Suddenly he was attacked by a huge
stag. He would have been gored to death if a
miracle hadn't happened. A wooden cross (or
holy "rood") appeared from nowhere. The king

grabbed it and beat off the stag. He founded the abbey on the spot. (Well, that was his story anyway.) Later history is not so holy. Mary Queen of Scot's favourite, David Riccio, came to a nasty end at the Palace. His attackers dragged him away from the Queen, threw him down the steps and hacked him to death.

Welcome to Scotland! Bonnie Prince Charlie danced the night away at Holyrood in 1745. To stop people seeing his bonny legs under his kilt he wore flesh coloured tights.

What's inside? The long picture gallery. It's long and full of pictures.

Can we come in? Walk this way. Paying visitors welcome.

Crumbly quiz question: What sight greets guests arriving at a Holyrood garden party in July?
a) Tubs of giant thistles.

b) Prince Philip playing the bagpipes.
c) The annual kilt twirling contest.

5 Kensington Palace
Where is it? London again. It's really lots of houses – one big royal apartment block.

House history? Dozens of famous royals have lived and died here. William III died at Kensington after his horse stumbled on a molehill and threw him. Queen Anne died here. King George II once had his silver watch stolen in the Palace gardens by a thief. Then he er ... died here. Despite its deadly record, modern royals like Princess Margaret, the Gloucesters, the Kents and Princess Diana have all lived at Kensington.

What's inside? The king's staircase has a *trompe l'oeil* (trick-of-the-eye) painting. As you go up you see courtiers staring over the balcony at you. They're watching in case you try to pinch the silver.

Can we come in? Oh all right then. Part of the palace is open to the public.

Royal verdict: "The aunt heap", Kensington was once home to many elderly royal aunts.

Crumbly quiz question: Princess Margaret first lived in apartment number 10. Why did the press call it "the doll's house"?

a) Because of her doll collection.

b) Because she looked like Barbie.

c) Because it's so small.

6 Sandringham House

Where is it? Deep in Norfolk. An ugly red brick mansion owned by the Queen.

House history? Edward Prince of Wales (later Ed VII) bought it for £200,000. He used it for holding wild houseparties. The train that delivered the guests from London was nicknamed "The Prince of Wales special". (The one that took them home was the Prince of hangovers special.)

It was also George V's favourite hangout. He made his first ever Christmas royal broadcast at Sandringham.

What's inside? The royals at New Year. The Queen pulled down 91 rooms in 1977. Now she's only got 270 to choose from. By spoilt royal standards it's a bit cramped.

Can we come in? Keep those turnstiles clicking. House and estate open to the public.

Royal verdict: "The place I love better than anywhere in the world." – King George V.

7 The Tower of London

Where is it? Don't ask stupid questions.

House history? More like grisly history. William the Conqueror built it. Henry III's house pets included lions, in case any uninvited guests turned up. Other kings have locked their enemies in the Tower or had them executed on Tower Green.

What's inside? Royals since Henry VIII have avoided living there (can you blame them?). Instead, the Crown Jewels were kept inside until recently.

Can we come in? "Roll up, roll up, have your photo taken with a Beefeater."

Royal verdict Don't ask if there's somewhere you can lay your head. You might not see it again.

LOOK WHAT I FOUND IN THE TOWER!

8 Windsor Castle

Where is it? London again? Wrong, Berkshire actually.

House history? Another one of William the Conqueror's building projects. After the Battle of Hastings he was very keen on castles to keep out his enemies. Many dead royals lie in the vault including George V and VI – the Queen's grandfather and father.

What's inside? The priceless royal art collection – Leonardo da Vinci, Holbein and all the other big names. You can also see Henry VIII's suit of armour (and get lost inside it).

Can we come in? Tickets sell like hot cakes.

Kindly don't mention hot cakes – there was a nasty fire at Windsor in 1992. Sorry.

Royal verdict: "Methinks I am in prison" –

King Edward VI, aged 12.

"This dear old glorious castle." – Queen Mary.

Crumbly quiz question: Which famous posh school lies just across the river from Windsor.

a) Sandhurst.

b) Eton.

c) Greyfriars.

4a) Tubs of outsize thistles – the emblem of Scotland.
5c) It was considered small, only ten rooms, hardly enough for a spoilt royal to swing a cat.
6b) He hated anyone to be late.
7a) The bloody tower – Why? Isn't it blooming obvious?
8b) Eton College. Prince Michael of Kent went to school there. He was once caned by his house captain for "mobbing in the corridors". (Like moping in the corridors only more noisy.)

Tiresome tourists

As we've seen most royal heaps and crumbly castles open their doors to tourists.

Why do they do this?

BECAUSE ROYALS ARE KIND AND HOSPITABLE ?

You're joking of course. Those crumbly castles cost millions to run. So the royals invite tourists to help pay the bills. More than 17 million foreign tourists flock to Britain each year. Almost half of them watch the changing of the guard at Buckingham Palace (though not all at the same time). Another two million queue to gawp at the Crown Jewels. So the Firm is doing brisk business. In a survey conducted for the *Daily Express* in 1992, most people rated tourism as the best reason for keeping the royal family. It came out top of the poll with 30%. Only 7% thought the royals' personal qualities made them worth keeping!

Ghosts and ghoulies

Many royal houses and crumbly castles are haunted. It's only to be expected really. British history is littered with kings and queens who came to a sticky end. Naturally spoilt royals aren't satisfied with just one life. They want to come back a second time to have fun haunting people.

Windsor Castle alone boasts enough spooky sovereigns to make up a football team. They include a little grey man, Elizabeth I, her dad Henry VIII and one of his headless wives, poor Anne Boleyn. Another is King George III. During his reign, George liked to rush to his window to salute the guards as they marched past. The officer in charge would always give the order, "Eyes right." A week after the king's death the guards passed the window again. There was the ghost of poor George at the window. The officer hesitated for a brief moment then gave the order, "Eyes right."

You think that's spooky? Listen to the tale of the Castle of Mey, owned by the Queen Mother in Scotland.

The green lady

It was a night when the moon was full. A mist was coming in from the sea. I was out walking my dog, Trixie. Suddenly she started to growl and the hair stood up on her back. I turned round and saw a lady. She was wearing a green dress that hung to her feet. In her hand was a lantern that swung in the wind. She gripped me by the arm.

"We must get away from here," she said. "Where is the carriage?"

I thought that maybe she was a foreign visitor and meant the bus. "You've missed the last one," I said. "It doesn't run after ten o'clock."

"We must run then," she whispered urgently. "If my father finds us it will be the death of me."

I was going to explain that I'd never seen her before in my life. I wasn't about to run away with a mad woman. And I wasn't eager to meet her dad either. But she had hold of my arm and was pulling me up towards the road.

"Come before it's too late!" she kept saying.

Just then a light came on in the castle. "That's odd," I thought. "I didn't think anyone was there at this time of night."

The woman saw it too and stepped back in alarm. She let go of my arm. "It's him. My father! He's coming for me," she said. Her eyes were wild and frightened.

The next moment she began to move towards the castle. It was as if someone was dragging her along, although I couldn't see anyone with her. She was arguing and crying.

I decided the poor woman needed a doctor and ran after her. But I'd lost her in the mist. Then I heard her cries echoing inside the castle walls. It was a sound to chill the blood. The castle doors were locked and there was no way in. I stood there for a long time, wondering what to do. Should I call the police or forget it and go home?

Suddenly Trixie began to bark. I looked up and saw a shadow at the highest window in the tower. A lady's shadow. The next moment I gasped in horror. The window was open and I could see a woman standing on the ledge. Before I could move or call out, she jumped from that dizzy height. I saw her fall down to the black rocks below. I rushed to where I'd seen her fall. Reaching the place, I searched the rocks. But the body had vanished. I could find no lady in green, no open window and no sign of life in the silent, gloomy castle.

Next morning, feeling a bit of a fool, I told my story to the sergeant at the police station.

"This woman. How was she dressed?" he asked.

"In green," I said. "A long green dress."

He nodded. "That would be the green lady. Lady Fanny Sinclair her name was. Daughter to the 13th Earl of Caithness who owned the castle."

"She was real then?"

"Oh yes. Fanny tried to run away with a servant lad. She was in love with him. But her father, the Earl, wouldn't allow it. He caught them trying to escape. He dragged Fanny back to the castle and locked her in her room. But he forgot the window. She leapt to her death from the top of the tower."

I stared at him open mouthed. "When did all this happen?"

"Hundreds of years ago, sir," smiled the sergeant.

"But ... I saw her, I spoke to her."

"What you saw was a ghost, sir," said the

sergeant.

"The green lady still haunts the castle, many a person has seen her. Maybe she thought you were her lover come to take her away at last."

That's what happened. Did I imagine it all? Or did I really meet the ghost of the green lady that dark night?

THE ROYAL GOODIES

Let's get down to business.

> HOW STINKING RICH IS THE QUEEN EXACTLY?

a) Comfortably off.
b) Fabulously rich.
c) *Loaded* with *lolly*?
The answer is:

SHH!

IT'S A SECRET

The fact is the Queen isn't telling. And by law, you can't make her.

Things are different for other world leaders like the president of America. Every year his tax return is published in the national newspapers. So everyone knows how much he gets paid and how much he has to give back in tax. In the Queen's case, no one knows how much she's worth. What's more she didn't pay a penny in tax until recently. When it comes to holding onto their lolly, royals have got it licked.

Many people claim the Queen is the richest woman in the world. Lots have tried to guess her wealth. In 1992, someone said it was £6 billion. That's £6,000,000,000,000.

Prince Edward, her youngest son, replied …

> If she's worth £6 billion I'd like to know where it is.

That's the problem with playing "guess what's in the Queen's piggy bank", it depends on the rules of the game.

Most people get paid a wage which is known as their "income". But what if you count your house, your clothes and your priceless collection of football stickers? The Queen gets paid an allowance every year by Parliament but she also has palaces, jewels, pictures and so on which belong to the State. So adding up her wealth isn't easy.

BREAK OPEN THE PIGGY BANK!

Counting the pennies

With all that lolly, does the Queen buy bags of new tiaras every week? Far from it. Most royals are stingy as well as spoilt. They know that if you look after the pennies the millions will look after themselves. Royals are famous for saving money any way they can.

Study the top ten royal tips.

Top ten money-saving tips

1 Keep strict accounts

As a child the Queen got a shilling (5p) a week pocket money. She kept detailed accounts of how she spent it.

2 Claim off the State

When Prince Charles was born in 1948, there were still food shortages after World War II. But if you had a baby you could claim free rations. Naturally the Queen wasn't going to miss out on a free offer.

She sent a servant to her local Food Office to collect a baby's ration book for free cod-liver oil and orange juice.

3 Collect the rent

Prince Charles could eat well on his rents from the Duchy of Cornwall. They include: a pound of pepper, caviar, a salmon spear and a leg of mutton.

4 Recycle your sequins

When her evening dresses are worn out the Queen has the sequins and beads removed. They are then sewn back onto her new dresses.

5 Cut down on loo paper

In 1892 visitors to Windsor Castle were surprised to find newspapers in the toilets. A little light reading? No, Queen Victoria was saving on loo paper. No one dared to complain about the bum deal.

6 Drive an old banger

For many years the Queen's personal car has been a 1971 dark green Rover. She says she aims to drive it until it gives up the ghost completely.

7 Recycle your hats

The Queen Mother tells her hat-maker to save any

old hats that can be used again. She has them re-trimmed with bows or feathers to match new dresses.

8 Always charge the public

In 1941 the royals put on a pantomime for a specially invited audience. The Queen was doubtful whether they should charge at the door.

"No one will pay to see us," she argued.

"Nonsense," replied Princess Margaret, "They'll pay anything to see us." The audience was duly charged 7s 6d (41p) to get in (quite a lot in those days).

9 Never waste a cigar

After his abdication, King Edward VIII saved his half-smoked Havana cigars to relight the next day.

10 Look after your pets

As a child Prince Charles once lost a dog-lead at Sandringham. The Queen sent him back to look for it. "Dog leads cost money," she told him, wagging a finger.

Terrible taxes
Quick royal quiz

Which of the following does the Queen pay?

1 Death duties.
2 Dog licences.
3 Telephone bills.
4 Income Tax.
5 Stamps.

Fab fashion

I don't believe in fashion, full stop.

Prince Charles

With all that lolly, the royals should be world leaders in fashion. The sad truth is that some of them are fashion disasters. Take the Queen – what's her most famous contribution to fashion? Headscarves. Her son, Prince Charles, is another fashion disaster. Even when visiting hot countries he wears a jacket and tie. Sometimes he even tucks the tie into his trousers. (If your teacher did that would you let them in the classroom?)

Whether they're in ski-pants or tweedy twin sets, what the royals wear is keenly watched by the press and the public. It's always been the case and royals down the ages have had a big influence on fashion.

Mind you, some of them had more taste than others.

Fab fashion – a short royal history
1 Eggy Bess

Portraits of Queen Elizabeth I show her looking every inch a queen. But Good Queen Bess had some barmy ideas on fashion. In Elizabethan days it was fashionable for women to have pale skin. (People would have thought getting a tan as stupid as rolling in a pigsty.) Queen Liz kept her skin pale by

107

whitening it. She used a revolting mixture of egg, powdered eggshell, poppy seeds, lead, borax and alum. It must have smelt terrible! Not only this, in old age she wore a huge red wig and padded out her mouth with cotton to hide her missing teeth. To crown it all the Queen was one of the first topless monarchs. In later life she had a habit of opening her dress to reveal her ageing bosom to everyone present.

On one occasion Elizabeth wore a shawl next to her skin. It was embroidered with a large black spider. The Queen was puzzled that none of her courtiers went near her, until she discovered the reason. They all thought the spider was real!

2 Strict Vicky

Queen Victoria, with her black dresses and high-necked collars, was as trendy as a funeral. In fact after her beloved husband Albert died she went into mourning for years. Albert had a few peculiar fashion habits himself. In bed he dressed like a baby. "He slept in long white drawers, which enclosed his feet as well as his legs, like the sleeping suits worn by small babies," wrote Victoria after his death.

In her younger days, Vicky was more inclined to cut a dash. Invited to Paris in 1855, she was keen to charm the elegant French. But she lacked any fashion sense. Victoria arrived carrying a large handbag, decorated with a great gaudy parrot. It was a gift, embroidered by her daughter. This was nothing to the little number she wore for the State dinner that night – a dress with big bunches of geraniums sticking out all over the place.

Victoria was ashamed of her podgy hands. To hide them, she wore rings on her fingers and even her thumbs. Unfortunately this made eating with a knife and fork rather difficult. The bemused French must have thought she hated their food – as well as dressing like a flower shop!

3 Trendy Eddy
Edward VII was the most fashionable royal of them all. Trendy Eddy wore the last button of his waistcoat undone. His pals noticed and soon anyone who did up all their waistcoat buttons was branded

NO, IT'S THE WAISTCOAT YOU LEAVE UNBUTTONED!

an old fogy. Eddie wasn't finished, he introduced the dinner jacket, the Norfolk jacket, the Homburg (a hat that looks like someone has punched it), knicker-bockers and the sideways crease in trousers. Eddy was one cool dude!

Edward VIII followed in his grandad's footsteps. When he quit the throne he turned to more important matters. Like trying to knot his tie. He perfected a new fat knot which became known as the Windsor knot. Tie-knotters everywhere rushed to their mirrors and tried to work it out.

4 Frumpy Fergie

Fergie, the Duchess of York, came in for a lot of stick in the press for her fashion taste. Poor Fergie was labelled plump and frumpy. One particularly nasty news editor said her stomach and hips had "a texture halfway between a satsuma and a helping of lumpy school custard". In fact Fergie was very

DETENTION

I TOLD THE DINNER LADY HER CUSTARD LOOKS LIKE FERGIE'S BOTTOM!

popular when she first married Andrew. She even

started a brief fashion for the Fergie bow, worn at the back of the hair.

5 Elegant Diana

A fairytale princess when she married Charles, Diana was the most-copied of royals. Thousands of women dashed to the hairdressers asking for the Princess Di look in 1981. Her elegant looks and fashion taste made her a target for photographers wherever she went. Diana appeared on the cover of fashion magazines all over the world and wore dresses designed by the great names in fashion like Dior and Versace.

Before her death in 1997 Diana sold some of her famous dresses for charity. The auction of gowns worn by the princess raised over £2 million.

6 Tweedy Lizzie

Our present Queen probably wouldn't bother with clothes if she didn't have to. That doesn't mean she'd go about baring her bosom like Lizzie the first. She's really happiest slopping around in tweedy skirts and jumpers. But being Queen she has to put on a show for the public.

The truth is she probably has more gear than any woman in the world. You've probably got a wardrobe or a few drawers for your clothes. The Queen has three whole rooms full of clothes in Buckingham Palace! But with all those clothes critics still reckon she's about as trendy as a teacher in a plastic mac.

Think you can do better? Be a fab royal fashion designer.

Trendy Queen kit

THE QUEEN SOMETIMES ONLY HAS 20 MINUTES TO MAKE A CHANGE OF OUTFIT. SOLUTION — ONE PIECE ZIPPER OUTFIT SHE CAN JUMP STRAIGHT INTO

SLEEVES HAVE TO BE LOOSE FOR FREEDOM OF MOVEMENT. THE QUEEN ONCE HAD TO KNIGHT A TALL MAN. AS SHE REACHED UP SHE HEARD A LOUD RIPPING NOISE FROM HER SLEEVE

112

HER MAJ'S FROCKS OFTEN BEAR
THE EMBLEM OF COUNTRIES
SHE'S VISITING. SPAGHETTI
FOR ITALY? STARS AND
STRIPES FOR USA?

 — SMALL HATS SO WE
CAN SEE HER FACE

GREY HAIR? WHY NOT REVIVE ROYAL
WIGS! IT WAS GOOD ENOUGH FOR
CHARLES II

SPECS — TOO OLD
FASHIONED. INTRODUCE
ROCK STAR SHADES

THE QUEEN WEARS
BRIGHT COLOURS SO
THAT SHE'LL STAND
OUT IN A CROWD.
HOW ABOUT A
MAN UNITED STRIP?

SHOES — HAVE TO BE
SENSIBLE SO SHE CAN
STAND FOR HOURS.
TRAINERS OR DOC MARTENS?

REVOLTING SUBJECTS

Sadly not everyone is a fan of spoilt royals. They're only jealous. Just because *they're* not the richest woman in the world.

These whingers are known as anti-royalists (not auntie royalists, they are the Queen's relatives). Anti-royalists hate the whole idea of royalty. At one time you could have easily recognized them. They would be walking around headless, after a trip to the chopping block. These days royals aren't allowed to go round slicing off their enemies' heads. Pity. So they just have to put up with the rude things people say about them.

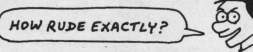

HOW RUDE EXACTLY?

Good question. Here are some famous royal critics and the things that they've said.

Rude royal critics
1 Whingeing Wells
H.G. Wells is famous for writing a story about a time machine. But he also made time to be rude to royals before it was fashionable.

He once said the royal family was, "Uninspiring and alien".

King George V replied ...

I may be uninspiring but I'm damned if I'm alien.

SHAME!

114

2 Irksome Altrincham

In 1952 no one dared criticize the Queen. So Lord Altrincham blamed her advisers instead. He said that they made her sound like, "a priggish schoolgirl, captain of the hockey team, a prefect and a recent candidate for confirmation."

Loyalists quickly leapt to the Queen's defence. The Duke of Argyll said of irksome Altrincham ... "I'd like to see the bounder hanged, drawn and quartered."

One Italian monarchist even challenged him to a duel.

Cheesed-off, Lord Altrincham gave up his title in 1963 and became plain Mr John Grigg.

3 Angry Osborne

The writer John Osborne, famous for his play *"Look Back in Anger"*, turned his rage on the monarchy in 1957. "My objection to the royal symbol is that it is dead; it is a gold filling in a mouth of decay."

4 Moaning Muggeridge

Journalist Malcolm Muggeridge was the first to compare the House of Windsor to a soap opera. His criticisms were actually as mild as soapflakes: "There are those who find the ostentation of life at Windsor and Buckingham Palace not to their taste."

All the same, royalists declared war on Muggeridge for daring to say royals were spoilt. He had dog-poo shoved through his letter box and was banned from appearing on the B.B.C. (A case of carpet smelly and no telly.) Muggeridge protested that he'd also said that the monarchy played a useful purpose. By that point of course no one was listening.

5 The blushing Beatle

Everyone's heard of The Beatles – the most popular pop group of all time, but did you know one of the Fab Four was rude to royalty? John Lennon handed back his M.B.E. medal to the Queen. He explained, "It was an embarrassment to me ... I don't believe in royalty and titles."

6 Whining Willie

The most persistent critic of royalty has been Willie Hamilton, M.P. Whining Willie kept up a one man crusade against royals in the House of Commons. In 1973 he proposed a motion to cut off the £92,000 a year paid to "the old lady" (his rude name for the Queen Mother). The motion was roundly defeated. Like John Lennon, Hamilton was against the Queen giving out honours. He complained, "When the Queen makes her sorties into the Commonwealth she hands out medals to every acolyte (toady) in spitting distance."

7 Pesky pets

Even pets have given spoilt royals the bird at times. The Queen Mother once came nose to beak with a talking mynah bird at a Sandringham flower show. She came off worst in the conversation.

Mad muggers

It's bad enough when your revolting subjects are rude about you, but royals have far worse things to worry about. In the past kings have been bumped off by their subjects. It's said that King James I was so scared of being stabbed, he wore padded clothes for protection. People said that as a result of all that stuffing he waddled like a duck.

Instead of padding, modern royals take bodyguards with them everywhere they go. You can recognize the bodyguards by the big bulges under their suit jackets. That isn't padding, those are their guns! Yet, even with all the security, some mad muggers have managed to get close to royals.

1974 – Princess Anne kidnap attempt!

A man tried to kidnap Princess Anne on her way back to the Palace today. The kidnapper swerved his car in front of hers and attacked two policemen who tried to protect the Princess. He wounded them both as well as the Princess's driver and a passer by, before being arrested. The attacker, Ian Ball, had planned to hold the Princess to ransom for £3 million. Her father remarked, "If the man had succeeded in abducting Anne, she would have given him a hell of a time while in captivity."

1974 – Loopy lieutenant leaps on Charlie!

Earlier today Prince Charles was set on by a potty lieutenant at the Portland Navy base in Dorset. The Prince was woken by a noise at two in

THANK YOU YOU

DON'T MENTION IT MENTION IT

THREE CHAIRS FOR CHARLIE...

the morning. When he poked his nose into the sitting room, an armed man jumped on him. Awakened by the struggle, Detective Chief Inspector Paul Officer came to the Prince's rescue. He was just in time to stop the attacker crowning Charles with a chair. Charles said he was most grateful to Officer Officer.

1981 – Queen draws blanks!

Shocked spectators at the Trooping of the Colour saw a man fire shots at the Queen. Her Majesty was riding on her favourite horse, Burmese, when 17-year-old Marcus Sarjeant stepped out from the crowd. He pointed the gun straight at the Queen and fired six shots. The crowd gasped. How could anyone be such a rotten shot that they missed six times? It turned out that the gun had only fired blanks. The plucky Queen calmed her startled horse and rode on

to complete the ceremony. Sarjeant was sentenced to five years in prison under the 1842 Treason Act. "If someone really wants to get me, it is too easy," said the Queen later.

POP!

GOD SAVE THE QUEEN

As it turned out she was right. Only the next year...

The Queen tells of her ordeal:

One was awoken just after seven o'clock in the morning. This was as usual. What not as usual was no sign of tea or the maid. Instead one was rather taken aback to find a man in scruffy jeans and T-shirt in one's bedroom. The intruder sat down on the bed. "Make yourself at home by all means!" one thought.

HELLO! IT'S SEVEN O'CLOCK

I SUPPOSE IT'S BETTER THAN WAKING UP TO RADIO ONE!

One couldn't help noticing he wasn't wearing any socks or shoes. One learned later that he had got in by shinning up a drainpipe. Then he removed his sandals and socks to walk along the corridor.

What was one to do? Scream? (Hardly royal.) Wrestle him to the floor? (Not in one's nightie.) Keep him talking till help arrived? The best plan of action. Smelly Feet introduced himself as Michael Fagan. He wasn't waving a gun or showing off his knife collection. The poor chap just seemed to want to talk about his family troubles. (One has enough of one's own!) Listening politely, one reached across and pressed the night alarm button. It's connected to the police control room and is supposed to bring a burly P.C. running at the double. Evidently it wasn't working. No burly P.C. No at the double. One thought quickly and rang the bedside bell. Would you believe it? No answer. The maid was obviously deaf and the footman was out walking the corgis. (One learned later that the only armed guard had gone off duty. Really! One might as well stand at the window with a big bullseye on one's nightie crying "Shoot me!")

Smelly feet was still talking. He asked for a cigarette. Ah ha! A chance to do a runner.

"You see there are none in this room, we will have some fetched for you," one promised him sweetly. Nipping out into the corridor sharpish, one at last found the maid. (Make a note to buy the girl a hearing aid.) At that moment the footman came back in with the corgis. Servants are like buses, never there when one needs one, then they come along in twos.

Eventually the footman and the maid managed to back my uninvited guest into a pantry. They kept him there well stocked with cigarettes. The police eventually arrived. One looked at one's watch. The whole ordeal had lasted eight minutes from the time one first called for help. Philip will throw an almighty wobbly.

One could have been lying dead in a pool of blood. Then what would the morning papers have said? (To say nothing of the cost of new carpets.)

121

Snivelling servants

Most of the time royals can ignore their revolting subjects. Subjects are there to cheer and wave when royals go past. Sometimes a few of them line up to meet the Queen. She shakes hands and says a few royal words to them. ("Who are you? Have you washed your hands?") But most of the time subjects can be kept at a safe distance. There is one exception – snivelling servants.

COULDN'T I DO WITHOUT SERVANTS?

Be serious. You can't possibly expect a royal to pour his own tea or get dressed by himself. Most royals haven't yet learned to tie up their own shoelaces! Servants are there to do it for them. Servants are of course a nuisance. They hang around in corners, and whine and snivel when you horsewhip them. Nevertheless, they are an essential part of the royal household.

If you want to be royal, you must learn how to deal with snivelling servants.

The royal household is organized on three levels. They are known as members, officials and staff. Members, such as private secretaries, are in the top drawer, officials are below them and staff get the rotten jobs like cleaning the toilets. (Except if you're the Groom of the Stole – more about him later.)

The Queen likes to have lots of servants, all with nutty titles. If you see a servant hovering at breakfast it could be the Lord Steward or a lady-in-waiting. Which one is it and what are they waiting for? You need to know before asking them for more toast and marmalade. It may not be their job in which case they will snivel in an unattractive manner.

Here to guide you through the maze, is a brief list of servants and their nutty titles.

1 The Lord Steward

Duties: Not a lot. Attends the Queen at big occasions like the opening of parliament. At state banquets he walks backwards ahead of the royal procession. Remember it's rude to turn your back on the monarch.

Don't say: "Watch out for the hole!"

2 The Lord Chamberlain

Duties: Organizing state visits and funerals etc. Like the Lord Steward, a champion backwards walker. Responsible for Queen's annual garden parties.

Don't say: "When are we playing pass-the-parcel?"

3 Master of the household

Duties: The head butler who handles the day-to-day running of the royal household. Has lots of servants with daft titles to run around after his orders. Six hundred meals are served every day in the palace so has to know his onions.

Don't say: "Bring me the bill, waiter."

4 The Travelling Yeoman

Status: Under the Master of the household.

Duties: Looks after all the royal luggage when the Queen is on a foreign visit. The royal cases are blue with "The Queen" printed in gold on them (just in case thieves find them hard to spot).

Don't say: "Who's bringing the old bag?"

5 The Yeoman of the Gold and Silver Pantries

Duties: Have a guess.

Don't say: "Yo man! Bring me some gold and silver".

6 The Groom of the Stole (or First Lord of the King's Bedchamber)

Duties: In George III's reign, the Stole in question was the king's close stool (or royal potty to you). The Groom was responsible for it's "cleaning and maintenance". No doubt he used the royal bog brush. Thankfully for the groom, the title survives but not his original duties.

Don't say: "I need a stool to sit on."

I BET NO ONE EVER STOLE HIS JOB...

IF THEY DID I'D KICK UP A STINK!

7 Keeper of the privy purse

Duties: Nothing to do with privies or potties this time. He looks after the Queen's piggy bank, including the money from the Duchy of Lancaster and the lease on the posh Savoy Hotel in London.

Don't say: "Lend us a pound." Say: "Lend us a million."

8 Master of the Queen's Game of Swans

Duties: The Royal swans were originally there to be scoffed. King Henry III and his mates downed 125 of them just for Christmas dinner in 1251. But commoners weren't allowed to tuck into roast swan. "Swannage" – helping yourself to the King's swans

– was a serious offence. The Master of the Swans now tries to look after them. He counts the number every year, before reporting back to the Palace. **Don't say:** "Anyone fancy a change from turkey this year?"

9 Silver Stick-in-Waiting

Duties: There to help another servant called Gold Stick. Gold Stick hangs around with his pal, Black Rod. Remember we met him at the State opening of parliament? Gold Stick has a big truncheon with a gold head to protect the monarch from would-be attackers. It works like this. Say an attacker with a knife jumps out at the Queen. Gold Stick comes at them with his truncheon. If they nobble Gold Stick then, never fear, Silver Stick-in-waiting is ... um waiting in the shadows to leap out and clobber them. Hurrah! The Queen is saved and the monarchy is safe. You see, all these snivelling servants are actually essential to have around.
Don't say: "My stick's bigger than your stick."

10 Ladies-in-waiting

Duties: There are ten of them. Some are duchesses and countesses who make excellent waiters. The top lady-in-waiting is the Mistress of the Robes who takes care of the Queen's fab fashion. She outranks the Ladies of the Bedchamber who are not to be muddled with the Women of the Bedchamber. What do they actually do? Things like answering the Queen's letters and looking after guests at royal bashes.

Once when Prince Charles was a tot, he pressed a

half-sucked sweet into the Queen's gloved hand. Unfortunately she was just about to shake hands with a reception committee. A lady-in-waiting nimbly leapt forward with a clean pair of gloves. That's what they're there for.

Don't say: "Are you waiting for me?" (They get confused.)

Nutty knights and dotty dames

Another problem with revolting subjects is that they may rebel. Lots of Kings and Queens of the past have wrestled with this question. King Charles I found his subjects so revolting that he fought a war with them. He lost the war and they chopped off his head to show they could do without a spoilt royal.

Fighting your own subjects may not be the best way to tackle the problem. So how do you keep them from rebelling?

1 Be nice to them (not easy for spoilt royals).

2 Give them some of the lolly you've got stashed away (expensive).

3 Hand out lots of dotty sounding titles.

Answer: *Number 3 obviously.*

Splendid. You're starting to get the hang of this. Handing out titles costs spoilt royals nothing. There are lots of titles they can give people and naturally they all have potty sounding names. Make your enemies a Knight of the Garter or a Dame Grand Cross. They'll be eternally grateful and never call you "snooty pants" again. The truth is most people are dying to be given a title by the Queen. Even Prime Ministers come over all weak at the knees at the thought of the Queen saying, "Arise, Sir Tony."

SO HOW DO I GET IN LINE FOR A TITLE?

As usual it's a crackpot business.

Knighthoods

It was William the Conqueror who first dreamed up knighthoods. He saw it as a good way of bribing powerful lords to support him. Charles I went even further. He actually flogged off honours for cash.

There's a story that James I was once so delighted with a loin of beef he had for dinner, that he drew his sword and knighted it. "Arise, Sir Loin," he said. And that's why you can order "Sir-loin" steak in a restaurant today.

AND I DUB YOU THE GRAND OLD DUKE OF PORK!

It's a good story but of course it's complete twaddle. Sur-loin is simply French for "the part above the loin". Today of course you can't get a title as a bribe or pay cash for it. Everything is strictly fair and above board. And there are never any favours handed out. The fact that people who give money to political parties end up with knighthoods is just a coincidence. (Honest.)

You might think the Queen decides who'll be handed an honour. In fact she only gets to do the prize giving. The list comes from the prime minister. But he doesn't have much of a clue about the names either.

THEN WHO DO I HAVE TO CREEP TO ?

Play the honours game

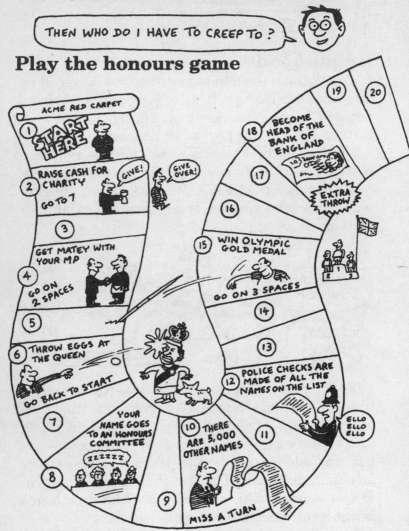

PS In case your moment in history gets forgotten, Buck House generously offers to let you have a video of the Queen knighting you – of course you'll have to pay for it.

THE ROYAL HEADLINES

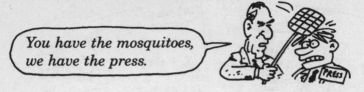

You have the mosquitoes, we have the press.

Prince Philip to the people of Dominica

If fame is what you're after, spoilt royals are never out of the spotlight.

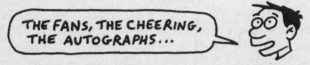

THE FANS, THE CHEERING, THE AUTOGRAPHS...

And of course the press. Just think. Reporters and photographers will follow you everywhere. They'll camp outside your house. They'll phone up your friends. They'll follow you to school. They'll pester your teacher to tell them about that time you got in trouble.

THEY WILL?

Of course. The press will want to know everything about you. Who's your favourite pop star? Do you have any pets? Do you sing in the bath? Do you pick your nose? (It's too late to stop now.)

Even when you're on holiday you won't be able to get away. The press will come with you. Just as you're changing into your swimming togs a camera will pop out and snap you. Next day everyone will be seeing a lot more of you on the front pages.

If you want to be a spoilt royal, it's impossible to keep out of the papers. The press are potty about the present royal family. And the royals are often mad about the press. The problem is that reporters just won't leave them alone! The papers' favourite story is spotting a royal acting spoilt. Royals behaving badly are guaranteed to sell millions of newspapers. As one newspaper owner once said: "News is what someone somewhere *didn't* want printed."

The press are always printing stories the royals don't want us to see. And if they can't find a true story, reporters can always make one up.

It's no surprise then that royals say rude things about the pesky press. Here are some of their remarks.

Raging royals quiz
1 Which royal made a right charlie of photographers when he announced his engagement, by saying: "May I take this opportunity to wish you all a Happy New Year – and your editors a particularly nasty one"?

2 Who yelled at the press at her Sandringham home: "I wish you would *go away!*"

3 Which rude royal, faced with hairy apes and crowds of reporters on the Rock of Gibraltar, asked, "Which are the monkeys"?

4 Which royal sister claimed, "I've been misrepresented and misreported since the age of 17 and I long ago gave up reading about myself"?

5 Which horsey royal said, "I don't fit into the slot they think I ought to"?

6 Which royal once got a passer-by to help her snatch the film from a press photographer's camera

Answers: 1 Prince Charles **2** The Queen **3** Prince Philip **4** Princess Margaret **5** Princess Anne **6** Princess Diana.

Polite press

The royals and the press haven't always been at war. Before the 1960s the press were terribly polite about royals. Some might say they were a bunch of creeps! Articles about the royals in the press sounded like a court diary...

> *Buckingham Palace, 9 June:*
> *The Honourable Lady Flatbottom today took tea with the Queen. They had a splendid spread of cucumber sandwiches with a Dundee cake to follow. Lady Flatbottom said afterwards, "The Queen was very nice. We talked about gardening. She is very fond of flowers."*

You get the picture. The idea of reporting the royals was to tell you nothing at all – except that the monarchy was a jolly good thing.

It was the same in the days of the Queen's grandfather. The press always showed great respect. A crisis only arose when George V was dying. A page from the diary of Lord Dawson, the King's doctor, would have made interesting reading.

Doctor's diary

The King is dying – but I do wish he'd get a move on. At this rate he will peg out after the morning papers have been printed. Think of the scandal – the King of England dies and it's left to the evening papers to tell the world! The shame of it! Naturally the passing of a king must be reported first in The Times, the only

newspaper read by people who matter.

Something has to be done. And as the King's doctor I think it's up to me to save him. The only way to preserve his dignity is to help the poor chap to go quickly.

Lunchtime – I have given George something to

speed him on his way. Coming into the dining room I picked up a menu card and wrote, "The King's life is moving peacefully to its close." The Times will be about to print the news tomorrow morning. Royal dignity has been preserved! God save the King! On second thoughts it's a bit late now.

The same polite treatment was given to the sensational news of the next King's abdication. Edward VIII was smitten with a lady called Mrs Simpson. But Mrs Simpson had been married twice before. And the king wasn't allowed to marry someone who was divorced. For a year Edward carried on seeing Mrs Simpson while not a breath of it was mentioned in the press. When a British editor got a photo of the king and Mrs Simpson together, they cut the king's girlfriend out of the picture!

It wasn't until a week before Edward abdicated that the story finally appeared in the English press. It must have been a shock to a lot of the nation, even though readers in Europe and America had known about it for a long time!

The foreign press were way ahead of Brit newspapers. They realized early on that gossip about spoilt royals sold newspapers.

In the 15 years after the Queen was crowned the French press printed:

- 73 reports that the Queen and Prince Philip were about to divorce.
- 63 reports that the Queen was about abdicate.
- 92 claims that she was pregnant.

Only two of these 228 stories turned out to be true! (That the Queen was pregnant, twice.)

Hello royals!

Today royal reporting falls into two types. In the blue corner are the royal fan-club. In the red corner are the royal ratpack. The royal fan-club is made up of glossy magazines like *Hello*. They adore the royals and love to show pictures of them dressed in their diamonds and tiaras. The ratpack are also known as the gutter press (because royals think they belong in the gutter). Their stories appear in daily newspapers like *The Sun* and *The News of the World*. Their favourite pictures are royals caught doing things they shouldn't.

Hello interviews are different. They are really a chance for the rich and famous to show off.

In 1990 *Hello* pulled off one of it's biggest scoops. It took us on a personal tour of Andrew and Fergie's new £5 million dream home. (Some people rudely called it a nightmare.)

If *Hello* did another interview with Fergie today it would still treat her like royalty. A gutter press interview would be a different matter. They'd be dying to ask lots of rude and awkward questions.

Try comparing the two imaginary interviews.

Hello interview

HELLO: Duchess, you've told your fascinating story in a book.

FERGIE: Yes, it's called *My Story* by The Duchess of York.

HELLO: Why did you write it?

FERGIE: You see, so much has been written about me which is untrue. I wanted people to know the truth. To hear my side of the story.

HELLO: Do you miss being part of our wonderful royal family?

FERGIE: There are obviously some people I miss.

HELLO: Like Prince Andrew? Do you think you made mistakes in your marriage?

FERGIE: Oh yes, I made mistakes but that's in all the past. I just want to get on with life now. I'm very busy. I write a column in an American newspaper and I just want to spend time with my beautiful children, Beatrice and Eugenie.

HELLO: They are utterly gorgeous.
FERGIE: Thank you.

HELLO: And may we add, you are looking completely stunning in that emerald dress with a pearl necklace.
FERGIE: Thanks. Thanks a lot.

HELLO: No, thank you so much for talking to us, Your Royal Highness.
FERGIE: (Dropping her voice) Actually I'm not your Royal Highness now. They took away my title.

HELLO: We know, but we still like saying it.

Interview for the Daily Scum

SCUM: Duchess you've written a book?
FERGIE: Yes, it's called *My Story*.

SCUM: Catchy title. Why did you write it?
FERGIE: So much has been written about me which is untrue…

SCUM: And you needed the cash, didn't you?

FERGIE: Well … I … of course the money came in handy.

SCUM: Handy? You were about £3 million in the red. How on earth did you ever go through all that lolly?

FERGIE: As a royal I obviously had a lot of expenses.

SCUM: Like your shopping expenses. On one trip to New York alone you spent over £3,000 on handbags, nearly £4,000 on Italian sweaters and the giant teddy bear cost…

FERGIE: Yes, well I'm sure people don't want to read my shopping list.

SCUM: Prince Andrew. Was it your fault the two of you split?

FERGIE: Obviously, I've made mistakes but that's all in the past now…

SCUM: Like that big mistake on holiday with your friend, John Bryan, the Texan millionaire. I'm sure you saw the photos in the paper the next day? The ones by the swimming pool.

FERGIE: I really don't wish to talk about that…

SCUM: What exactly did the Queen say about those pics? I bet she did her royal nut!

FERGIE: Really! I'm not putting up with this anymore.

SHE STORMS OUT

Royals on the box

LIGHTS, ACTION... ME!

It isn't only the newspapers who are crazy about the royals. Television is just as royal potty.

In a way spoilt royals have only themselves to blame. They were the ones who first let the cameras into Buckingham Palace. The Queen thought appearing on TV every Christmas was a good way to speak to her subjects. But once TV got a taste of the royals, it wanted more and more.

Royals on the box – the highlights
1952 The Queen's Speech
The Queen's first televised Christmas broadcast. A gripping drama with the Queen reading her speech from a cue board next to the camera. Afterwards, she said to the producer, "It's no good, I'm not a film star." But millions tuned in for the repeats every Christmas.

1969 The Royal Family
Half the country peeped into the lives of Britain's most famous family and saw them as they'd never seen them before. Prince Philip rowed a boat! The Queen expertly barbecued a sausage! Prince Charles expertly snapped a cello string into brother Edward's face!

Twenty-three million people tuned in to see royals at work and play. Thirty million had watched England win the World Cup in 1966. Royals were almost as popular as football in those days!

1986 Highgrove House

The programme where Prince Charles showed us round his garden and talked to plants. Prince Charles went on to make several other TV programmes about his pet subjects. One programme moaned about the mess architects have made of our towns and cities. Another moaned about the mess we are making of the environment.

1987 It's a Royal Knockout!

The game show to end all game shows. *It's a Knockout* was a popular TV show in the 1980s. Two teams competed in daft games against each other. In a typical game contestants wore giant heads and wobbled round an obstacle course, bumping into things. Buckets of water, falling over and cheering were the main ingredients. It was rather like a giant TV circus.

Why on earth did the royals get involved in the programme? The idea sprang from the head of Prince Edward. He imagined a royal knockout, with lots of famous stars joining the young royals. It would raise lots of money for charity – and people would see that royals weren't stuffy after all.

The four teams are each led out by a waving royal – Andrew, Fergie, Edward and Anne. Sarah calls her side 'The Big Bad Blues' team.

All star teams including: singers Cliff Richard and Tom Jones, racing driver Nigel Mansell, TV stars John Cleese and Anneka Rice, film stars Christopher Reeve (Superman) and John Travolta.

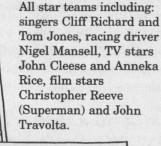

Andrew gets carried away and sets off a cannon. It singes the eyebrows of presenter Stuart Hall

BOOM!

Press tent. Prince Edward ticks off reporters for being a bunch of moaning minnies.

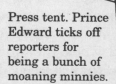

HAVE FON OR I'LL SULK!

The games – stars dressed as giant vegetables try to knock each other down. Spoilt Royals cheer their teams on as "non-playing" captains. Fergie, eager to get into the action, pelts Prince Andrew with fruit.

143

1992 Elizabeth R

Made to showcase 40 years of Elizabeth II sitting on the throne. Starring: The Queen – with her family playing all the walk-on parts.

In 1993 the writer, camerman and soundman for the programme all popped up in the New Year's Honours List. Just a coincidence of course!

A big mistake?

When the first royal blockbuster *The Royal Family* was made, some said it was a mistake. One of them was David Attenborough, the TV wildlife presenter, who knows all about endangered species. He told the producer: "You're killing the monarchy with the film you're making."

Attenborough said the royal family were a bit like tribal chiefs in their hut. A certain air of mystery had to be preserved around the chief. If any of the tribe ever saw inside the chief's hut then the air of mystery vanished and the tribe would fall apart. Was he right? Has TV poked its nose in too far and been the downfall of the royals? It's true our attitude to royals has changed. We see them very differently nowadays from 1952 when the Queen was first crowned. At that time they seemed like characters in a fairy tale, today they sometimes seem more like characters in a soap opera!

The press and the princess

On 31 August 1997, the world discovered the news that Diana, Princess of Wales, had been killed in a car crash.

During her life Diana's face had sold millions of

144

newspapers and magazines every week. But fame came at a high price. From the day she met Prince Charles, Diana was hunted by the press wherever she went. On the night she died her car was being chased through the streets of Paris by a pack of "paparazzi" photographers.

Who was to blame?

Was it the driver of her car? He had been drinking and was driving at 95 mph when the car entered a tunnel and crashed.

Was it the paparazzi? They were chasing Diana's car on high-speed motorbikes at the time of the accident. Several witnesses claimed they drove dangerously close to the car.

Was it the newspaper editors? Some of them paid huge sums of money – up to half a million pounds – for a single photo of Diana. Without them, the paparazzi couldn't exist.

Or was it everyone – everyone who ever bought a newspaper or looked at a magazine that contained reports and pictures of Diana?

1 Paparazzi are photographers who work for themselves. They sell their pictures to the highest bidder.

ENDANGERED ROYALS

By the end of the 20th century only five monarchs will be left in the world. The kings of England, hearts, diamonds, clubs and spades.

King Farouk of Egypt

Don't bet on it

King Farouk may have been hasty. The Queen will need to live until the year 2015 to become the longest reigning monarch in British history. (She'd be almost 90.) But even if she lasts that long, will the monarchy itself survive? Or will Elizabeth II be known as Liz the last?

One Brit is betting against it. In 1993, a man placed an £8,000 bet that the monarchy will bite the dust by the year 2000. The bookmakers, William Hill say, "We don't know who he is but he didn't have big ears and a posh voice." They shortened their odds against the royals not seeing out the century from 100 to one to five to one. That means they think there's a one in five chance that spoilt royals may be gone by the year 2000.

WE COULD NEVER DO WITHOUT ROYALS!

Could we? It's an interesting question. What would the future look like without them? Maybe something like this:

146

Britain in the next century

THE NEW PRESIDENT OF BRITAIN MOVES INTO BUCK HOUSE

I'M THE KING OF THE CASTLE!

THE QUEEN AND HER FAMILY LEAVE BY THE BACK DOOR

SPARE SOME CHANGE, MATE?

WINDSOR CASTLE IS SOLD TO HOLLYWOOD

GEE! DID ROBIN HOOD REALLY LIVE HERE?

THE CROWN JEWELS ARE FLOGGED OFF

SUITS YOU, SIR

THE QUEEN COLLECTS HER PENSION AT THE POST OFFICE

CASHIER

AND FOUR STAMPS WITH ME ON, PLEASE

PENSION

PRINCE CHARLES RUNS A GARDEN CENTRE

HELLO PLANTS, HELLO FLOWERS

ZZZ

Royals for the chop?

The future for spoilt royals looks dicey.

Royals may say they've seen it all before. Charles I lost his head and England did without a king for 11 years from 1649–60. But people got bored being ruled by Parliament. It was no fun without a king so they brought back Charles' son to be Charles II.

Things don't look so rosy for Charles III (as Prince Charles would be known). The 20th century hasn't been a good one for royals. When Queen Victoria died in 1901 almost every European country had its own royal. Most of them were relatives of Victoria's son, Edward VII – "the uncle of Europe". Uncle Eddy could fill a royal club with his European relatives alone.

Then something terrible came along. It was called the First World War. For the spoilt royals of Europe it meant a great clatter of crowns hitting the deck.

It was curtains for the Austrian-Hungary kings, the German Kaisers and the Russian Tsars. The Shah of Iran and the Emperor of China were next to get the boot.

Today royals are fast becoming a dying race. Are the Windsors of England next for the chop? In the press, on TV and even in the House of Commons the arguments rage back and forth.

Queen today, gone tomorrow?

Is there any future for Britain's royals in the next century?

Labour M.P. Ken Livingstone said, "I think the royal family should be left to self-destruct."

Even the editor of *Burke's Peerage* (a guide to royals and aristos) is gloomy about the future. "If the royal family doesn't change many aspects of its style, it will simply disappear like its relations across the continent."

In many ways it's up to us to decide. You and me. Prince Philip once famously said that if the royals were no longer wanted they "would go quietly".

There are three choices really. Keep them, sack them or make them change. Which would you vote for?

1 Carry on Royals

This view says things are fine as they are. Royals may have slipped on a few banana skins recently but that's nothing new. We've had them for centuries and we're not going to change them now.

The last prime minister, John Major, supported this view. He said the royals were "a very precious part of our life – a rock of stability in a changing world." He *would* say that though. No leader wants to go down in history as the prime minister who got rid of the royals. Even Margaret Thatcher didn't try that and she talked as if she was royalty herself!

So carry on royals? The trouble is that the public have got fed up with the royals lately. When Windsor Castle was damaged by fire in 1992 a £40 million appeal fund was started. Five months later how much do you think the British public had coughed up?

a) £25 million
b) £2.5 million
c) £25,000

2 Bye bye royals

Should the royal family be scrapped? Those who think so are called republicans. Republicans don't run pubs (those are publicans) they drink to the day that we can sack all royals.

One famous republican is Labour M.P., Tony Benn. He has even gone as far as writing a bill to get rid of royals. He called it The Commonwealth of Britain Bill. If Benn's bill ever became law this is what would happen:

1 The Queen would be dismissed as head of State and replaced by an elected president.
2 The House of Lords would get the boot. They'd be replaced by an elected House of the People.

3 We'd vote for two MPs instead of one. One male and one female.

4 The honours system would be scrapped for something fairer.

5 MPs, judges and generals would swear an oath of loyalty to the State instead of to the Queen.

Tony Benn introduced his bill in to the House of Commons in 1992. It was chucked out without even a discussion. It seems Britain isn't ready for a Republic. Not yet, anyway.

3 Bicycling Royals

There is a third choice. It is to keep our royals but to make them change. Instead of spoilt royals we could have bicycling royals.

Queen Beatrice of the Netherlands invented bicycling royals. As a schoolgirl she cycled every day from the Palace to her local grammar school. The sight of a royal on a bike was thought so amazing that people started talking about the bicycling royals of Europe.

Now she is grown-up, Queen Beatrice is still pretty different from our own queen.

- She pays the same taxes as everyone else in Holland.
- She pays her own electricity bill.
- Her fleet of cars consists of two Ford Granadas.
- She will retire at 60 to let her son become king.

She is very popular with the Dutch.

Other European royals also try hard not to be spoilt. The Queen of Spain makes do without ladies-in-waiting. The King of Norway walks around without a bodyguard. While his palace was being redecorated he lived on a humble dairy farm outside Oslo. (Though he drew the line at delivering the milk to his subjects.)

Lately there have been calls for our royal family to be more like the bicycling royals of Europe. Prime Minister Tony Blair thinks change is the way forward. He wants the royals to modernize. They're seen as stuffy and out of touch by many people. In a 1997 survey, 81% of people agreed that royals "should become more informal and less concerned with preserving their traditional ways."

What might happen if we went down this road? Maybe girls would succeed to the throne on an equal basis to boys. The Queen could end up paying all the same taxes as everyone else. Already she has lost her private yacht. Many of the trappings of royalty might follow. Perhaps one day she'll even ride to open parliament on her bicycle.

Tough job

Will the royals last well into the next century? Will Britain become a republic or will we have our own bicycling royals? You'll need a crystal ball to know the answer. One thing is certain – the years ahead will be tricky for spoilt royals. We expect a lot of them. We want them to be royal but not spoilt. We like them to ride in golden coaches but not to spend too much money. We want them to behave with dignity but not to be stuffy. In fact we'd like them to behave like the kings and queens in fairy-tales.

It's no easy job being a spoilt royal these days. Think you could do better? Apply for the job!

Dear Lizzie,

    I hear you've been having one or two problems lately. You've been Queen nearly fifty years now. Fifty not out is a good score, you deserve a holiday. Of course someone would have to keep the throne warm while you're away. And I happen to know just the right person.... ME!

    I love dogs and dressing up. Also my Dad says I'm a natural at spending pots of money. I don't mind travelling all over the world or having to eat whopping great dinners given in my honour. In fact I'll do such a good job people won't even notice you're gone. Just say the word and I'll pop down to the palace tomorrow.

Your humble servant

Dan (the first)

The Knowledge

Awful Art by Michael Cox
In this imaginative guide, you'll meet rich artists, poor artists, dead artists and artists who made an exhibition of themselves. Find out about some forgers and fraudsters, and how to create your own priceless masterpiece. PLUS are you the owner of an artistic temperament?

Mind-blowing Music by Michael Cox
Tune in to all sorts of cool musical happenings, from the birth of the blues to the amazing invention of a sound recording machine, and get into the groove with mind-blowing musical instruments. PLUS how to become an overnight pop sensation!

Smashin' Fashion by Michael Cox
This go ahead guide will kit you out from tip to toe. Try on a hat that started a riot, slip on some pointy shoes that are three times longer than your feet, and meet the fashion designer who made rubber, zips and safety pins fashionable. PLUS design your own smashin' fashion collection!

Foul Football by Michael Coleman
This kickin' guide tackles everything you
need to know ... from mean managers and
rotten refs to top teams, faithful fans and all
the cracking competitions, including events at
wonder-foul Wembly!

The Gobsmacking Galaxy
by Kjartan Poskitt
Jump up and down with excitement as you're
whisked away on a grand tour of the solar
system, where you'll go skiing on Mars and
meet the sad creature from Pluto. Plus ... find
out what happens when a bloke called Sid gets
too close to a black hole.

Groovy Movies by Martin Oliver
Go behind the scenes with this star-studded
guide – meet anxious actors, dastardly
directors, get animated with an A–Z of cartoon
capers, and see if the groovy movie screen test
sets you on the road to stardom.